# Driftwood
# and
# Amethyst

# Driftwood and Amethyst

## Kate O'Brien

| Library of Congress Control Number: | | 2011912954 |
| ISBN: | | |
| | Hardcover | 978-1-4653-0223-6 |
| | Softcover | 978-1-4653-0222-9 |
| | Ebook | 978-1-4653-0221-2 |

This book was printed in the United States of America.

Revision Date: 08/07/2014

**To order additional copies of this book, contact:**
Xlibris Corporation
0-800-644-6988
www.XlibrisPublishing.co.uk
Orders@XlibrisPublishing.co.uk
301573

*To Mum, Dad, Max and Harry,*

*Thank you for helping me find my silver lining.*

# CHAPTER 1

ophie Bird woke to hear the cries of seagulls outside her bedroom window. She smiled to herself as she opened her eyes and looked out of the window to see the bright lemon sun against a sky of hazy turquoise. Sleepily, she sat up and moved to the window where she could see the boarding house's back garden below, a pretty maze of rose trees, clematis archways and fruit trees. The Sandy Stop Guest House was one in a row of tall red-brick terraced houses on the seafront, each with matching postage stamp gardens front and back, dusted with daisies.

Her bedroom was also a mass of tiny flowers covering the pink walls, pink curtains, pink bedspread, and even pink lampshades—not really Sophie's cup of tea! But that was all part of coming away on holiday, Sophie had reminded herself when she had seen her room the day before. This was the first real day of her holidays, in this sleepy seaside village tucked away on the Yorkshire coastline.

She tied her dressing gown tightly around her and pulled her chestnut hair out from under the collar. Her toes sinking deeply into the soft rosy carpet, she tiptoed out to the bedroom next door. Sophie and her mum had come away with Aunt Penny and Cousins Danny and Nina. Danny was her best friend, and they had been looking forward to this holiday for months. Looking inside the identical floral pinkness of the room, she was greeted by unmade, empty twin beds. Sophie turned and ran downstairs in leaps of two steps at a time.

'Good morning, lazybones!' her mum called out as Sophie entered the dining room. Luckily, there were only a few people already sitting down at the small dark polished tables, but Sophie still blushed, sleepily. The dining room walls glistened white with a grand gloss fireplace on one wall. Sophie's toes sank once more into the carpet as she sat down and poured tea from a white china teapot into a dainty matching cup.

'We've just been discussing what to do today,' her mum started, tucking an auburn spiral behind her ear. 'We quite fancy looking around the old shops. What would you like to do?'

'I don't like shopping,' moaned Nina. She was only seven years old, and Sophie was already fed up with her grumpiness.

'We can't stay on the beach all day!' laughed Sophie's mum. 'We thought it might be nice to explore our surroundings.'

'Oh, leave her, Jen. She's having one of her days, I think,' Auntie Penny replied.

Old Mrs Dawson, the landlady of this fine establishment, brought in the first round of breakfast—a selection of small, boxed cereals.

'Good morning, my dears,' she said as she walked to their table.

'Hello, Mrs Dawson,' Sophie called. 'How are you?' Sophie always asked this as she didn't really know what else to say, and Mum was always reminding her to be polite.

'I'm fine, thank you, my dear,' Mrs Dawson smiled. 'A little stiff this morning, but that's the price you pay for dancing all night!'

Everyone laughed politely. Sophie chose a chocolatey cereal and poured milk over the small light brown pieces, watching them closely as the chocolate seeped gently into the milk.

Mrs Dawson seemed a really sweet old lady, Sophie thought, the type from picture books and fairy tales of long ago. She had gentle, pale blue eyes and light wrinkled skin that showed smiley lines around her mouth and eyes. A tiny woman dressed in black, she wore her long white hair in a bun pinned at the nape of her neck.

Sophie remembered the day before when they had first met. The sweet smell of lavender had been the first hint of her as they had stood in the entrance hall of the guest house. Mrs Dawson had seemed overjoyed that she, Danny, and Nina had come to her boarding house. She'd been quick to say she had been a schoolteacher many years ago at the village school by the cliffs and had retired to run the boarding house they had come to. She had added that the school was now closed, as there were no children left in the village anymore, at which Sophie had sighed a rather large sigh. Not having other children round her might be a drag, but at least she had Danny and Nina around her. Danny was really funny, and she was sure they would have a pretty good holiday all the same.

'We're thinking of going to look at the shops today,' Auntie Penny said. 'We quite fancy having a wander off the beaten track, looking at the older shops on the backstreets.'

Mrs Dawson looked quickly around at the children, and Sophie saw a flicker of a frown pass across her face. She smiled, but this time her eyes didn't twinkle as usual. 'Oh, you'd be better staying in the main town,' Mrs Dawson started. 'Those shops aren't really very interesting for such grown-up children like you.' This was directed at Sophie and Danny. Danny grinned at this, but Sophie caught his eye knowingly.

'I want to play on the sand,' Nina whined again.

Mrs Dawson walked around to Nina and tousled her hair. 'Of course you do, darling,' she replied. 'Stay on the main streets and by the beach. The children will have a much better time there.'

Sophie looked up, trying to read Mrs Dawson's eyes as she spoke, but the old lady turned away.

A breakfast followed of warm eggs, sizzling hash browns, runny beans, and tinned tomatoes for Sophie. She turned up her nose at

Danny's plate of pink bacon and speckled sausages, as she preferred to eat just eggs and beans being the vegetarian in the family, but they both tucked in, hungrily. Breakfast was soon over, and Sophie went upstairs to get ready for a typical seaside day out.

Sophie decided to speak to Danny about Mrs Dawson's comments as soon as they reached the beach. She had noticed something in the old lady's manner when talking about the backstreet shops—it may have been that there really wasn't much of interest there, but surely, that was for them to find out, wasn't it?

The morning was spent in a number of tatty souvenir shops and ice cream stalls along the seafront. Nina ate more ice cream than Sophie thought was possible for someone so short, but Nina seemed well enough on it. At the post office, Danny bought his favourite comic, as was his weekly tradition, and Sophie bought postcards for her three best friends back at home in London. Amrita, Jess, and Harriet were sorely missed and 'Wish you were here' was a complete understatement. Without them, she would have to rely on Danny to keep her entertained, as the gang of girls together were a force to be reckoned with back home. She knew she was missing out on bike rides, picnics, and digging for ancient relics in the park behind their estate, but she knew better than to hanker after something she couldn't have right now. They'd all promised faithfully to have a bike ride in the woods when she got back followed by a picnic in the park and a proper catch up.

Mum gave her three first class stamps, the boring ones with no pictures, and after buying three sticks of rock to take home for her friends, she met her mum and the others outside the shop. She would write her postcards later, she decided, when something hopefully would have happened worth writing home about.

As they started walking, Sophie discovered that they were going to spend the day on the beach after all. The beach was nice, but Sophie's mum and Auntie Penny were real sun worshippers and this could end up being a daily ritual. Sophie pointed out her concerns to her mum at the first possible opportunity.

'You have been pestering me to go to the seaside for ages, Sophie. Now we're here and you want to stay away from the sea! We're going to the beach and that's final. This holiday cost a lot of money. Me and your Auntie Penny want to enjoy ourselves too.'

Sophie didn't understand why Mum was being so bad-tempered. She was aware that the holiday had been expensive, what with the boarding house, train fare, blah, blah, blah. But they were all supposed to be having fun, not just the grown-ups.

Sophie and Danny walked along together in silence.

# CHAPTER 2

Mum and Auntie Penny set up their camp for the day the minute they arrived at the beach. Brightly coloured towels, an icebox full of drinks and sandwiches, wedged with the sandy sun cream bottles inside. It was a beautiful day, the sun scorching down from a bright blue sky, eased occasionally by a refreshing salty breeze. The mums rubbed sun cream into every visible body part, helping Nina as she stood, arms outstretched like a statue.

Sophie looked around to see that they were the only family on the beach. An elderly couple walked hand in hand along the seashore as their dog chased a gnarled piece of driftwood that they threw repeatedly in to the sea. Apart from them, there was no one else in sight.

After a lunch of sandy sandwiches, Danny and Sophie played football with wet towel goalposts at each end of the sandy pitch, with the centre and penalty areas carved deep into the sand with driftwood left by the dog's earlier game. They were both on the school football team back home; Danny in goal and Sophie in defence. Here, though, they played all positions and raced up and down their pitch, kicking the sand up as they ran.

'Sophie!' came a scream from the beach towels.

Sophie and Danny stopped and looked over to where their mums were sitting, now waving their hands and rubbing their arms frantically. Sophie and Danny ran over.

'The wind's blowing, and your game of football is kicking up too much sand. We are covered!' They were right. Mum and Auntie Penny had started to resemble breadcrumb-coated fish fingers.

'Well, what else are we going to do?' Danny asked. 'We've built sandcastles and played in the sea all morning!'

'Something that doesn't involve kicking sand all over us,' Auntie Penny replied, lying down again with her book. Auntie Penny was set to do nothing but read romantic novels and develop her suntan this holiday, and Danny could see it was no use.

Sophie tried her mum. 'Mum?' she started.

'Sophie, your Auntie Penny is right. Go and play somewhere else.'

Danny and Sophie walked a little further down the beach and sat down. They played hangman, scratching in the sand with their prized piece of driftwood for a while, rather half-heartedly. Sophie then started building up picture collages with the tiny pink and white striped shells she had found, while Danny added to them with seaweed and colourful pebbles. Before too long, they had created a fantastic mermaid with a seashell, pebble and sand body, seaweed hair and a seashell face. Danny had found one of those spiral shells for the nose and a long pink seashell, which had a bottom and top half, joined delicately along the side. They stuck it in the sand half open to make the mermaid's mouth. Sophie ran to get her camera and took a photo, with Danny sitting cross-legged pulling a stupid face as he always did in photos. They admired their work for a while, before deciding to call her Arial after 'The Little Mermaid'.

Nina ran over to see what they were doing. 'What is it?' she whined screwing her nose up and tipping her head to one side.

'A masterpiece,' Sophie answered. 'But you can see that, can't you? I heard you were really good at art.' She raised her eyebrows, daring Nina to argue.

'Oh yes, yes. It's really good.' Nina looked a little bemused, as Sophie and Danny looked at each other and laughed.

'Come on, squirt,' Danny said, pushing Nina's shoulder. 'Looks like they're packing up.'

Sophie looked over to where their camp had been for the day. It was now a series of bags and boxes. The area where they had stayed looked ruffled and untidy, scattered with half finished castles, deeply dug holes, and scrawling finger drawings.

The three children ran back to the camp and trudged back to the guest house laden with sandy buckets and spades, towels, and oily carrier bags.

After rubbing their arms and legs free of sand, Sophie and Danny joined their mums and Nina in the dining room for their evening meal. The tables were set with the already familiar china and heavy cutlery.

Sophie tapped her knife and fork together. 'Do you think we're eating with real silver tonight?'

'Yeah, Sophie—very likely.' Danny smiled, sarcastically, pointing out the words 'Sheffield Stainless Steel' written down one side.

Sophie had ordered vegetable lasagne. This was her favourite meal, but she had quickly realised that this was the only 'vegetarian alternative' on Mrs Dawson's menu. She now suspected it would be her staple diet for the whole week. As everyone else tucked in to fish, chips, and peas that evening, Sophie savoured her meal, as she was sure she would soon be sick to death of it.

After their first day of sea air, Sophie felt quite tired. She tried to watch Yorkshire Television for a while, as it was always quite exciting to see what was different on the telly when you were away from home, what with no satellite or cable channels to choose from.

But before long, her eyelids felt heavy. After saying goodnight and heading upstairs, she changed in to her pyjamas and snuggled down in multi-coloured layers of sheets. Briefly, Sophie looked up out of her window. The sky was a clear dark blue and silence echoed in her ears. Steadily, she drifted off to sleep.

# CHAPTER 3

Sophie awoke again to the cries of seagulls and watched a misty morning forming beyond her window. She looked at her watch, which was resting on the bedside table. Only a few minutes after seven o'clock, it read, and dawn had broken, the hazy morning light gently ebbing into her room.

Stretching, she went over to the window and looked down at the garden below. As she rubbed her eyes, Sophie focused on two figures stood together under a sprawling tree laden with delicate cherry blossom. They were partly hidden behind a wooden archway covered in pink roses, but one of the figures she recognised instantly as old Mrs Dawson. Her hair was pinned back in her usual tight white bun, and she was dressed in her usual black. Sophie watched her talking to a boy, perhaps about eleven or twelve years old, who was eating a large piece of bread or cake held tightly in both hands. Watching the two as they stood together, deep in conversation, she smiled at being part of this meeting, as Mrs Dawson rubbed the young boy's arm affectionately. Sophie moved closer to the window and rested both elbows on the wooden window sill. As she moved, the boy gestured upwards, and Mrs Dawson turned to look. As her eyes met Sophie's, Sophie pulled away, guilty of being caught watching something private. Mrs Dawson smiled and waved, but Sophie hid herself quickly.

'Are you awake?' a voice whispered. Sophie turned to see the sleepy face of Danny at her door.

'I've been up ages,' Sophie replied. She looked back down into the garden, but it now stood empty.

'Let's go down for breakfast,' Danny said from the door. 'I'm starving.'

They were pleased to discover that they were the first two in the dining room that morning. Sitting at the table where they had eaten the previous evening, they could enjoy a brilliant view of the sea. Mum and Auntie Penny walked in soon after, followed by Nina and Mrs Dawson.

'A gorgeous day for the beach!' Auntie Penny exclaimed as she sat down next to Sophie. 'What do you say?'

Sophie looked at her mum open-mouthed but was met by raised eyebrows and the irritated flap of a clean white napkin as Mum placed it on her knees.

'Fabulous.' Sophie picked up her napkin and flicked it back at her mum before, too, positioning it on her lap.

After breakfast, the five figures trooped down to the beach. Again, the bay was empty and so the camp was set up in its usual place, by the steps up to the main street. Mum and Auntie Penny passed around cream then lay down to 'soak up the sun' as they put it.

'Put plenty on,' Auntie Penny called, throwing the sun cream at Danny. 'I don't want you all looking like lobsters!'

After stripping off to their costumes, Sophie and Danny striped their arms and legs with the purple cream and rubbed it in gently, giving their arms a violet glow. Lumbering down the beach, arms outstretched, they moved like sea monsters returning home. At the point where Arial had been created yesterday, the sand lay in ripples from a gently retreating sea, not a trace of seaweed or shell left behind.

'The tides,' Sophie remembered. 'It's something to do with the moon. They come in and go out again every day,' she sighed loudly, sitting down in the sand.

Danny joined her. 'All that work too. I could swear!'

They both laughed and spent the next few moments digging their names in the sand.

'I know,' Sophie said standing up, 'let me bury you!'

'No way!'

'Oh, come on, Dan, then you can bury me.'

'You'd better dig me up after!' he giggled, as he lay down.

Sophie began by pulling sand over Danny's body from the sides and soon had covered him completely, leaving only his face clear.

'Hang on a minute,' she said, 'I've got an idea!' Sophie ran off to collect stones and seaweed. She placed seaweed around his head, then giggling, placed two large pebbles on his chest.

'What a babe!' she screamed, then ran off, laughing.

Danny looked down and shouted, throwing off the sand and running after her. 'I'll kill you!' he yelled. They both ran into the sea, Sophie still screaming. Danny soon got his revenge, grabbing Sophie by the shoulders and dunking her under the water a few times.

Underwater, time seemed to stop. She opened her eyes and saw her hair floating out in front of her before her eyes shut from the bitterness of the sea salt. After choking twice, gasping up to the surface, Sophie spluttered a salty 'sorry!' and the matter was forgotten.

They spent the final part of the afternoon swimming in the shallow water and in splashing each other. Looking over to the sand they could see Nina making her millionth sandcastle, while their mums lay like oily chicken drumsticks, occasionally moving to chat or turn over a page of their books.

When Sophie and Danny felt sick from swallowing too much saltwater, they came shivering out of the sea, acting the parts of their evil sea creatures again, stomping up to shore. They contemplated making a merman to keep Arial company when the waves would wash him seaward, but after looking around for a new stock of seashells and pebbles and finding very few, they decided not to bother.

'We could go for another ice cream,' Danny suggested sarcastically.

'Funny.' Sophie grimaced. Then a thought struck her. 'Why don't we go and explore? Let's see what is so dreary about the old backstreets.'

'Okay,' Danny agreed, rather reluctantly. 'If they let us,' he said, motioning over to where their mums lay. It would be difficult, being in a new place and being let off the leash for an hour or two, but at home both Danny and Sophie were in their final year at primary school and were allowed a little freedom around their home streets. Of course, they knew their home town well and only really went to the park and the woods beyond Sophie's estate, but they always got home on time and rarely ventured further than they should.

Danny and Sophie walked over to the camp, kicking sand up at each other as they walked but stopping before they got too close. They needed to stay in their mums' good books.

'We thought we might go for a walk,' Sophie started.

'Yeah,' added Danny, 'to the main shops. We thought we might have another ice cream.' He smiled at Sophie who managed to keep a straight face. If she ate another ice cream this year it would be too soon. After three days on holiday, she was sick of the things and was looking forward to working her way through the various ice lollies, brightly coloured and offering promises of fruity stripes, beaded toppings, and chocolate coatings.

'Can I go?' asked Nina, standing up and pulling at Sophie's arm. 'I want another ice cream, Mum.'

Sophie looked at her mum, pleadingly.

'No, Nina, you're too young to go with them. I'll pop up and get us all an ice cream in five minutes; I just want to finish this chapter.'

She turned back to them. 'Stay on the main front, and don't wander off too far. You're old enough now to have a bit of space, is that okay with you, Pen?'

Auntie Penny smiled. 'Stay with Sophie, Danny. And be back here in one hour, okay?'

Mum could be so cool when she wanted to be.

They dressed quickly and, after pushing their sandy feet into their even sandier trainers they ran up the steps on to the main street, after looking fleetingly at their mums and Nina. Nina was still making sandcastles, but a little more aggressively now than before.

# CHAPTER 1

Although the main street seemed quite busy with old couples carrying shopping bags or sitting on wooden benches reading their newspapers, the arcades played to almost empty halls, while a few old ladies sat dotted around, making their fortunes on the penny machines. The children walked along the seafront, looking out at a distant flashing lighthouse and the faint lines of circling seagulls over what may have been a trawler further out to sea.

'So, which way?' Danny asked as they crossed the main road.

'I don't know! This is new to me, too,' Sophie laughed. 'Shall we start with an ice cream?'

They laughed and carried on their way. After deciding to walk away from the main road but keep to the bigger streets, they felt secure in their plan. They knew they couldn't get really lost, as the seaside town they had come to was very small, but they wanted to feel safe, all the same. At least the main part of town was busy, and this way they'd be able to turn back onto the main street without losing their bearings.

Away from the main street, it was rather quiet, with only a few old folk wandering along the cobbles with the odd string bagful of shopping.

After five or ten minutes, Sophie started to wonder if this was such a good idea. They had seen nothing but a few old men in neatly pressed suits who were returning from collecting their groceries. The houses stood like soldiers standing to attention, their paintwork chipping, yet their gardens carefully tended and bordered with a smattering of what looked like pansies in pinks, yellows, and purples, although Sophie could never be sure. All flowers looked like pansies to her. They reminded her of the colours found in the sticks of rock here, striped and pastel, softening in the heat.

Danny, however, wasn't so easily put off and was enjoying the freedom. Sophie wondered if he was allowed out much where he lived, in the city with streets teaming with the older kids from the local comprehensive. Mum was always asking Auntie Pen to move nearer to them, but for now they just spent every holiday and quite a few weekends squeezed into their terraced house with the three children sharing Sophie's room, Danny and Nina making do with sleeping bags on the floor. Sophie smiled to herself and decided to let him have his moment, as it must be difficult if the only time he had to himself was playing football in his backyard. Maybe Auntie Penny was a bit over protective, but Danny was more than a bit immature, Sophie reminded herself. Mum had said that girls grow up much faster than boys. That much was true, and Sophie smiled to herself again.

Danny knelt down on the pavement and picked up a small chink of silver. He had just found an old 10p piece and was rubbing it clean with the hem of his T-shirt. 'Look at this!' he exclaimed. '1972! That was ages ago!' After waving it in front of Sophie's face so fast that she could barely focus, he pushed the coin deep into his jeans pocket and turned to face her.

'Shall we go back or what?' she asked. 'There's nothing much here. We could go and have a look at the arcades?'

'No way! This is great! No, parents, no, Nina. We'll go to the arcades later when we've got some proper money off Mum, stupid. I don't think the machines take ancient treasure!'

Sophie shook her head wearily. 'I don't mean that, silly, I've brought a couple of pounds with me—you can borrow some if you like.'

Danny walked on, his mind made-up.

Sophie sighed. 'Well, okay, I suppose we've got loads of time left. If we don't find something to do soon, we'll go back to the arcades. Or I could buy you an ice cream!'

They both made retching noises, placing their fingers down their throats and then continued their walk along the cobbles.

They soon came to a turn in the road that led them further away from the beach. Although they had initially decided to stay only one or two roads away from the beach, they carried on without discussion. The streets were becoming quieter, with only a couple of ladies, with faces wrinkled and brown like old tea bags, wandering past them. The road turned again, which made Sophie and Danny stop.

'We must remember how to get back,' Danny said, his adventurous streak leaving him for a moment.

'We know just to stay on this road,' she reminded him, her orienteering skills somewhat better practised than his, she was sure.

They continued walking; now taking care only to walk on the small flagstones and not between them. Nothing had been said, but they played this game carefully, as if their lives depended on it. Their journey took them along many more streets of neatly matching houses. These were fronted by paved chessboard fronts dotted with potted plants of blush pink and custard yellow. The air was still, warm and heavy.

Suddenly, Sophie looked up from her feet. To the right of them, a little way down the road, stood a small row of shops. Each one was painted a different colour, which had faded and chipped away over the years, as the sea breeze and sand had tormented them. Sophie nudged Danny and he too looked up.

'Here we are!' Danny cheered excitedly. 'Now, this is more like it. Let's go and see what all the fuss is about!' He sounded like someone who had something to prove. This adventure of course couldn't become a damp squib, as it had been his idea. Although she had first suggested it, he had taken it on as his own mission and had continued this painful exercise in order to show her he was right. He would make it a spectacular adventure regardless of what they managed to find, she was sure about that. That was boys for you.

# CHAPTER 5

ophie gazed down at the row of tatty shops, then looked at Danny with a note of despair. 'Danny, there are four shops. We have wasted nearly half an hour getting here. One of them looks like a chemist—let's just go!'

Danny was not so easily put off. With his chest jutting out, like a little robin redbreast singing his cheerful song, he was optimistic. 'We're here now. Come on. Let's at least have a look round.'

Sophie didn't really mind, but certainly didn't share his enthusiasm. He thought he was on the brink of some great discovery and was desperate to make this holiday memorable.

'Okay,' she agreed. 'Ten minutes, tops. Then we must get back.'

'Deal,' he smiled. 'You've got some money, haven't you? We could spend it here!' he added, pulling her jacket sleeve as he marched ahead of her. Sophie didn't want to spend her money on toiletries or cough sweets, that was for sure.

The row of shops looked as though they had stood there for a hundred years. Sophie had been right; there was a chemist, one of the old-fashioned styles with jars of stripy sweets on shelves above the counter and a set of brass weighing scales in the window. Maybe they could have a look round, after all.

But on closer inspection it was dark inside, and after trying the door, they realised that the chemist was closed. A little handwritten sign in the window read

*Closed on Tuesdays*

'Great,' muttered Sophie. 'We've walked all this way, and the only interesting shop is shut!'

Sophie and Danny walked on to the next shop. In the window lay a scattering of dead flower arrangements in faded blues and creams. Danny made some joke about them needing watering, and Sophie forced a laugh, annoyed at their wasted journey. Again the inside seemed dark, and when Sophie pushed the chipped salmon pink door, she saw a little handwritten sign, which read

*Closed on Tuesdays*

in the same handwriting as before.

The third shop had at one time been a bakery, but the lack of a window display told them that this had been closed down long ago.

'This is ridiculous!' shouted Sophie, throwing her hands up in despair. 'Everything is shut! No wonder, Mrs Dawson told us not to come here!'

Danny wasn't listening. He had walked to the final shop and was stood pressing his outspread hands on the glass, his nose millimetres away from a similar fate. The shop appeared to be closed, but a warm amber light glowed from inside, and Sophie walked steadily to where Danny had stopped.

She turned to face the windowpane. The window was filled with dolls dressed in beautiful costumes from many different periods of time and from many different countries. She could see a Victorian girl, her dirty blonde hair in pigtails dressed in a blue-and-white sailor suit, wearing tightly laced black patent boots. Nearby hung an Indian boy with short shiny black hair in his best red silk salwar kameez. When Sophie looked again she realised that they were puppets, their wrists and ankles pierced with silver wires. These wires hung from gnarled wooden sticks, old driftwood like those they had played with earlier on the beach. These were obviously for someone to move the puppets with, to make them dance or nod their heads, if they were ever allowed down from their hooks. Sophie swallowed as she looked at each doll, their eyes sad and empty, fixed on her.

Two puppets sat together, their heads resting on each other, wide blue eyes gazing out at Sophie. They were curiously similar, their curly auburn hair styled identically, with blue satin ribbons. Sophie carefully inspected their outfits of cream and blue flowered dresses with the same lace edgings at the neck and cuffs. Tiny white satin shoes dressed their feet, with covered buttons on the strap, their legs delicately crossed at the ankles. The girls were alike in every way, giving the impression of mirror reflections.

'This is amazing,' Danny whispered. Sophie wasn't sure why he was whispering, but she thought he sounded a million miles away. Sophie shook him gently.

Danny looked at her, mesmerised by the window display and she smiled.

'Come on, then,' she said quietly, 'let's see if there's anybody home.'

But as Sophie went to try the door, she saw the now familiar sign which read, just like the others

*Closed on Tuesdays*

and she pushed the door in annoyance.

To her surprise, the door opened easily without making a sound. As she turned to pull Danny inside, she saw he was still looking at the puppets in the window.

'Danny,' she whispered, not sure now why she was also whispering, 'It's open.'

Danny turned and followed her in without saying a word. They stepped into a dark cavern of a room, which certainly did seem lit with an amber glow.

Once inside, the door closed behind them. Sophie turned to see that Danny had pushed it shut, a habit he had from living in a large cold house with his mother. She thought about opening the door again, panicking for a moment as she tried to make sense of her surroundings, but Danny stood between her and the door, and she knew better than to start an argument right now.

Sophie shivered, as the room was particularly cold, and her eyes strained to adjust to the light. Her nose tickled the air thick with dust released from wood shavings that crunched gently underfoot.

Puppets hung from every shelf and filled every space on the walls, hung from old nails and hooks haphazardly around the place. It looked like a collection that had grown too big, puppets crammed together, and reminded her a little of her grandmother's hallway, the ad hoc arrangement of family photos, squeezed together as children grew older and sent latest photos, the rogues' gallery growing larger than the space she had appointed. A steady pathway led from the doorway to an old wooden desk at the back of the shop, wooden shavings trodden down, worn away as the tread of feet had created its own natural trail. Sophie swallowed as she realised, her stomach tightening, that she felt quite nervous. Moments passed as they stood like statues in the doorway of the shop. Sophie began to hear the quiet of the room, her ears deafened by the silence, until it became almost unbearable. She turned to Danny in a bid to leave when a sound came from below the floorboards, from some kind of basement room.

Someone or something was steadily climbing the stairs. They quickly turned to face each other, their eyes wide and faces serious. Cut into the opposite side of the room was an arched stone doorway, from where the footsteps were coming.

As the tread of the squeaking stairs became louder and louder, the two children took tiny, silent footsteps back towards the main door. Sophie had hold of Danny's jacket and pulled him back with her as she grasped back into the darkness for the door handle.

A shadow fell across the arch, tall and elongated with long fingers outstretched towards them. Not waiting to meet the owner of that shadow, they scrambled out of the door noisily and ran out into the street, their trainers beating fast over the cobbled stones, faster and faster, until they reached the familiarity of the seafront. Holding on to the chipped blue railings that separated them from the steps down to the beach, they leaned forward, gasping for breath.

# CHAPTER 6

'Perfect timing!' Mum called as she looked up to see them.

Sophie and Danny stomped wearily down the rocky staircase without saying a word. They both took a couple of stripy canvas bags each, filled with sandy buckets, spades, and wet towels.

'So what did you two get up to?' asked Auntie Penny as they began walking back up to the guest house.

'Not much,' Sophie lied, looking across to Danny for support. His face was flushed, and he looked over without speaking, his breath still a little strained from the run.

As they entered the guest house in single file, Danny turned to Sophie. 'We must go to the puppet shop tomorrow, just like today. We have to go back.'

'Danny, the place is spooky,' Sophie started, 'you won't get me in there again.'

'We've got to see who works there,' he ordered. 'Just think of the stories we can tell everyone when we get home!'

She followed Danny reluctantly to his bedroom. Nina remained downstairs, having her toes cleaned of sand and seaweed.

'I wonder who it is,' he whispered, looking to the sea from his window.

Sophie was becoming more and more concerned by Danny's interest, especially when she was so against the ideas—they were usually together on most things. They stood together in silence watching the seagulls circle in the sky.

'I got a bad feeling about that place,' Sophie whispered. 'I'm not sure that going back is such a good idea.'

'Well, I'm going again.' He frowned, looking out past the glass. 'Maybe even tonight. You do what you want.'

They made their way silently downstairs for dinner.

Dinner passed by with little excitement. Danny seemed much more himself by the time the meal was over, and Sophie felt able to talk to him again as they left the dining room for their bedrooms.

'If you want adventure, then we could have a look at old Mrs Dawson's school tonight instead of the shops,' Sophie whispered. 'We haven't been there and it's not far.'

Danny frowned and pushed past her on the stairs.

'Oh come on, Dan,' she continued, 'it'd be much more interesting—I'd love to see how ancient the old school really is!'

Danny looked back at Sophie and then smiled. 'We come all the way here to escape from school and now you want us to visit one that isn't even ours!'

Sophie could see the twinkle in his eye return and smiled back at him. She had secretly hoped this would take Danny's mind off the puppet shop. 'Come to my room now.' She smiled. 'And we'll work out when to go.'

With Sophie's bedroom door securely closed behind them, they sat down on the bed to make plans.

'They mustn't know we've gone,' he started when a moment or two had passed. 'We need to leave the beds so they look like we're asleep in them.'

'I've seen that done in films!' Sophie laughed. 'Make the pillows into a body shape underneath the covers, and they'll never know.'

And so it was decided. As soon as their watch hands turned to midnight, they would meet outside on the landing.

'We'd better synchronise our watches,' Danny added, putting on his secret agent voice for full effect.

Sophie then planned how to get to the village school, marking their journey on the local map her mum had bought on the previous day. The blue marks indicated a walk that would take them over three or four miles of open fields up to the cliff top where the school stood.

With Danny gone, Sophie squeezed her pyjamas on over her day clothes and slipped into bed. Her watch read 9.30 p.m. as she glanced at it over and over again, her eyelids becoming heavier and heavier. Realising that she would never be able to stay awake until midnight, Sophie quickly set her watch alarm for 11.55 p.m. and settled her head down into her pillow. Within moments of snuggling under her blankets, she was fast asleep, dreaming of the sad faces of the puppets, the mysterious figure coming up from the basement, and the little boy standing alone under the apple tree.

A faint bleeping sound dragged her away from troubled dreams. She opened her eyes to find the room dark and full of shadows. Sleepily, she peeled off her pyjamas to reveal her day clothes, and as planned, she placed the pillows in her bed to make a sleeping 'Sophie shape' under the sheets. Standing back to admire her work, she pushed her bare feet into trainers and silently left the room.

Danny was already out on the landing when she shut her door behind her, and they tiptoed carefully down the staircase together, as one. The front door of the guest house was securely bolted, but with a little determination and Sophie's soundless work, they were soon outside the building with the heavy oak door pulled securely back into its frame.

The sky was a clear dark blue, and the two children stood for a moment looking up at the many stars that lay speckled across the sky. Without speaking, they looked at each other and then ran in hushed tiptoe movements down to the main road.

# CHAPTER 7

hich way now?' Danny whispered, when they were far enough away from the house to stop and plan their next move.

'We need to follow the sea road, until it curves towards the countryside. There's a short cut across the fields and then we'll see it.' Sophie was pleased with the route she'd planned. Long division and grammar may have always been a problem for Sophie, but she had always been able to find her way using a map. Auntie Penny had once said that Sophie must have been a homing pigeon in a past life.

They could hear the sea steadily washing over the sand beyond the wall as they walked quickly along the sea road. The village was silent, and Sophie looked around her, amazed at how different the village looked at night. The sea had a magical quality as it mirrored the starry sky above it, giving the impression of diamonds floating on an ocean of blue velvet.

Time seemed to evaporate as they walked and walked. Hours could have been minutes; minutes could have been hours as they continued to tread along the sandy roadside. Sleepiness and darkness rolled together to make the two walk as if in a trance, following the road as it suddenly turned away from the sea and up towards the countryside as Sophie had predicted. This shook them from their dream, and they began to discuss the next stages of their adventure.

'Up here are the fields. The school is at the other side of them, above the cliffs,' Sophie explained.

Overgrown hedgerow surrounded the first field, with a roughly cut stile fixed at one corner. This allowed the only entrance, partly hidden by the hedge, holly and a few nettles thrown in for good measure.

'This hasn't been used for ages!' Danny noted as he watched Sophie scramble up the wooden structure. 'Be careful up there! Don't fall!'

Sophie carefully placed her foot on the step on the other side of the stile. 'It's just a series of steps, Danny, do what I do.'

Sophie winced as she spoke. Her legs and arms were scratched and nettled as she pulled herself free and jumped down into a freshly ploughed field.

Danny followed cautiously but fell forward as he landed. In the darkness of the night, Sophie saw his hands were covered with beads of blood from many thorny scratches.

'Are you okay?' she asked, pulling Danny up.

'I think so,' he replied as he rubbed his hands clean.

The two trod silently across the field lit only by the light of the moon. They left a trail as they walked, sinking into the muddy soil with each footstep.

At the other side of the field was yet another stile, matching the first in every way.

As Sophie climbed, hedgerow branches scratched her face. She brushed her face and placed her weight on the stile. As she tried to climb over, her jeans caught on twisting thorns, and her jumper became tangled with brambles hidden in the hedge. Sophie pulled and pulled from the thorns and brambles in all directions. With one final mighty tug, she pulled herself free and jumped over the stile.

'Mother Nature is not making this very easy for me!' she joked as she picked herself up from the floor.

Danny followed with less difficulty, and Sophie watched as she rubbed her stinging scratches.

Back on the main road, she could see that the school was quite close, as it towered above the village cottages nearby. As they walked towards the impressive building, Danny pointed out that it was boarded up and probably had been for some time. A small church sat next door with a graveyard front garden and a silver cross on its roof, glinting in the moonlight. At every window and door of both buildings, dark sheets of hardboard were nailed tightly into their frames, suggesting there was no way in or out.

As they stood, Sophie spotted two doors, one at each end of the school. Above each door read a carved sign in the stone: *Boys* then *Girls*. The school was surrounded by tall black pointed railings, which would make it difficult to get in.

'Let's have a look round,' she said, returning to her usual volume for the first time since they had left the guest house.

Danny nodded, and they walked around the outside of the building. It was made of old dark grey stone with a matching grey slate roof. At one side of the school, they found another stone carving in the same style that read:

$$St.\ Joseph's\ School$$
$$Est.\ 1885$$

Railings towered above them, and after unsuccessfully attempting to squeeze themselves between the thin black bars, they kept walking until they were at the very back of the school. The railings continued until they came to an ornate, rusting gate.

Both children seized the gate and pushed. Nothing happened. There didn't seem to be any lock or fastening so they pushed again. Slowly, the gate opened and led them into the playground. Here, the school seemed even bigger. Their footsteps became increasingly timid as they walked over to the building. The windows were too high to look into, and from what they could see in the darkness, the glass was too dirty with layers of webs and dust to see through anyway. They walked with their bodies against the walls and moved along steadily by pushing their hands along the brickwork, somehow protected from the silent shadows.

Soon they came to the entrance that boys had used years before. This was blocked by hardboard, but on closer inspection, Sophie could see that the board was hanging loose.

'Look!' she called as she pointed to the doorway.

They moved closer, and Sophie put her hands underneath the bottom of the board. Danny helped to pull it away from the door frame. As the board creaked upwards, Sophie strained her eyes to see through the darkness of the corridor within. The children moved closer on hands and knees, as their fingers skimmed the old polished wood of the floorboards within. A dusty smell accompanied the gloom, like in ancient churches or derelict houses.

As her eyes adjusted to the shadows, Sophie gasped. A startled face stared back at them, hazel eyes wide and terrified, his pale skin stained with dust and tears. Hair fell wildly around his face in a dirty mass of chocolate brown, and he froze, crouched down just a few feet away from them, his breathing quick and frightened. Sophie pulled back in shock and then calmed herself by forcing a few heavy breaths in and out. She opened her mouth to speak, but the child jumped up and ran away down the corridor behind him. Clambering in after him, she heard a noise behind her. Danny was running back towards the gate they had come through.

'Danny!' she called as loudly as she dare.

He did not respond but continued running, until he had disappeared into the night. Sighing, half in annoyance and half in relief, she ran after Danny all the way back to the guest house.

# Chapter 8

The next morning, as soon as breakfast was over, Sophie and her family started off for yet another day at the beach. As the towels and canvas bags were placed on the sand for the day, Sophie ran barefoot down to the seashore. The white edges of the waves tickled her toes as she stood for a moment with her face raised up to the sun. She tightly screwed her eyes shut, and they flooded with bright red light as the sun glared through her eyelids. Neither child had mentioned the school since they had run from it the night before, but the sequence of events was still in the forefront of Sophie's mind. She was sure Danny felt the same way.

Auntie Penny had bought a beach tennis game for Danny and Sophie to play with, which began the morning well. The two played competitively for over an hour. The sun shone, and the brightness of the day steadily began to blot away any anxiety still remaining from the night before. After a lunch of cream cheese and cucumber sandwiches, Sophie and Danny went for a walk along the sea edge. Sophie's toes sank deep into the oily sand beneath the water, often met by comforting seashells and slimy strands of seaweed.

'I want to go and speak with Mrs Dawson,' Sophie told Danny. 'I think I should tell her about the little boy in the school.'

Danny frowned at Sophie and then kicked at the white surf of a new wave rippling onto the shore. 'Don't do it, Sophie. She'll tell our mums we were there.'

'I don't think she would. I like her,' Sophie confided. 'She might be able to help him.'

'Sophie, grown-ups are grown-ups—and you know what grown-ups are like. She'll say something to them, she's bound to, and then we'll be watched like hawks for the rest of the holiday.'

'I trust her. She seems all right, and I think she needs to know.' Sophie's mind was made up. She pushed Danny to try and lighten the moment.

He shook his head and turned away.

Sophie ran over to her mum and Auntie Penny. 'Mum, I'm not feeling so well. Can I go back to the guest house?'

'You'll be fine,' Mum replied, without leaving her magazine for a moment. 'Just sit here and rest. You've been hurtling around the place all morning. You've worn yourself out, that's all.'

Sophie sighed, 'No really, I need to go back.'

Nothing.

'Mum, I feel really sick. Let me go.'

'You do look a bit peaky,' Auntie Penny added, looking out above the rim of her sunglasses. 'Do you want me to come with you?'

'No, I'll just go and sit with Mrs Dawson.'

Sophie's mum stood up. 'No, if you're not well, I'll take you back. I'll have a word with Mrs Dawson and make sure she doesn't mind babysitting you while she gets on with her jobs.' She stood up. 'For heaven's sake, Sophie, you do choose your moments.'

Back at the Sandy Stop Guest House, Sophie's mum spoke with Mrs Dawson as Sophie was left in the television room. Soon, they both appeared at the door.

'Mrs Dawson has kindly offered to keep an eye on you while you sit and watch the telly. I think you'll be fine when you've had a couple of hours in front of daytime TV,' she added, winking at the landlady.

Sophie smiled as weakly as she could and looked back at the television. A man and woman smiled out at her from the screen, turning charcoaled bits of meat on a barbecue. Sophie heard the door close behind her mum and breathed a sigh of relief.

'Cup of tea?' Mrs Dawson called as she popped her head around the door.

'Yes please,' Sophie replied, settling back in the squashy flowered armchair.

Mrs Dawson returned with a tray of white china cups, saucers, and a matching teapot, the familiar soft scent of lavender accompanying her, which Sophie found warm and comforting.

'Let's see.' Mrs Dawson smiled as she poured two steaming cups of the brew. 'Are you going to tell me what's really wrong with you this afternoon?'

Sophie looked up to see Mrs Dawson's pale blue eyes twinkling at her.

'Nothing,' she started, but when her eyes met Mrs Dawson's, Sophie smiled in embarrassment. Lying had never been one of Sophie's strong points.

'Shall we try again?' Mrs Dawson asked warmly. She smiled again, and suddenly, Sophie realised she had nothing to fear.

'Mrs Dawson,' Sophie began, 'something has been on my mind.'

'I know, Sophie. Just say what it is you need to say.'

Sophie took a deep breath and spoke. 'I saw the little boy in the garden.'

'Yes, my dear, and I waved to you. I remember.' She took a drink of her tea, a cue for Sophie to do the same.

Sophie put her cup carefully back in its saucer and spoke again. 'Does he live with you?'

'No, my dear,' Mrs Dawson answered quietly. 'He stays nearby and visits me often.'

She placed her hands together and rubbed a beautiful purple stone set in a silver ring that shone from her finger. Mrs Dawson saw Sophie's interest. 'Amethyst. It helps me see more clearly,' she laughed to herself.

Sophie was intrigued with the way Mrs Dawson spoke. She'd never met anyone like her before. A wall clock framed with carved wooden vines ticked noisily, accentuating the silence.

'The little boy,' Sophie managed to say, her heart thumping heavily on her ribcage, 'does he live in the school?'

'The school is a safe place where, yes, he has stayed,' Mrs Dawson said slowly. She paused for a moment, turning her cup, examining the remaining tea leaves. 'There is much you don't know about this place, Sophie, and when you arrived here, I hoped and prayed you would not have it to discover.'

Sophie frowned and shifted uncomfortably in her chair. 'Who is the boy?'

Mrs Dawson looked at Sophie sadly. 'A lost soul, my dear. I do what I can. I wish I could do more.'

'What has happened to his parents?'

'Gone. Vanished into the ashes of time as most of us do.'

'Dead?'

Mrs Dawson nodded. 'This village once had many places of danger, and the school was the only safe place for our children. Its church and grounds are consecrated, holy, blessed. Sadly, we were unable to keep them there all hours of day and night.'

Sophie was unsure what she was being told and why Mrs Dawson was telling her. She half expected her to laugh at any moment and tell her she was only joking.

But instead, Mrs Dawson tidied away the cups and stood up. 'Let's wash these few things, shall we?' she added, and so, Sophie followed her into the back of the house.

The room they entered was Mrs Dawson's flat, a main room that housed a dark carved table with four matching chairs, squashy pink sofa, and two more oak doorways to what Sophie thought must be the bedroom and bathroom. In a far corner, a white porcelain sink and draining board sat under a hanging frame of pans and silver cutlery. On every part of the wall hung framed black and white photographs from long ago, cards and messages, poems and dried flowers tied with coloured ribbons. Sophie paused to look more closely.

'Are these your family?'

'Yes . . . and dear friends from many moons ago. They are all I have, and my memories,' she added softly as she walked over to the sink.

'Have you always lived here?' Sophie asked, fascinated by the room and the objects it held.

'For many years. A small part of my life was happy here. But much of it was troubled.' She gazed around the walls. 'The pictures serve to remind me of happier times.'

Sophie didn't know what to say. 'I'm sorry,' she finally muttered. Sophie had never seen before the sadness in Mrs Dawson's eyes. She looked troubled and seemed preoccupied, in her own little world.

Mrs Dawson smiled and wiped her hands on her apron. 'Let's leave these dishes. I think there's a film you may enjoy.'

They walked back to television room, and Sophie sank back in her chair.

As she left the room, the old lady paused at the doorway. 'Remember the dangers of the village, Sophie. There have been difficult times here. Do come and talk to me, I will always be here.' And with that, she left the room.

# CHAPTER 9

Sophie settled back, a little confused by her sudden change in mood, yet relieved to be away from the situation.

The afternoon passed as she watched black and white images of war-time families flash across the screen.

The family sat quietly at dinner that evening, all but Sophie red faced and shining with lotion. Nina's freckles were out in force, and she looked even younger as a result.

Danny had seemed very serious on his return and obviously had something on his mind. Sophie knew that the boy at the school had frightened him, and he had refused to talk about it at breakfast.

As Auntie Penny and her mum started planning their evening television, Danny nudged Sophie gently.

'I think we should go back to the puppet shop tonight,' he whispered, without looking up from his dinner plate. Sophie was shocked into silence and finished her meal without another sound. Neither child spoke again, until they ran upstairs after excusing themselves from the table.

At the top of the stairs, Sophie pulled Danny towards her. 'I spoke to Mrs Dawson today. She said there are dangers here. Perhaps we shouldn't go out at night again.'

Danny folded his arms. 'Well, I'm going. It can't be any freakier than the school!'

'I don't know, Dan, after what Mrs Dawson said, I'm starting to feel a bit weird about this place.'

Although Sophie didn't want to betray Mrs Dawson's trust, she needed to keep Danny safe. 'It's just something she said. I'm never normally spooked, but she was really serious!'

Danny gave her a look and turned away. 'Whatever. I'll go on my own.'

'No, Danny,' Sophie started, 'I don't think it's safe to be out at night—we wouldn't do it at home, so why here?'

Danny pushed open his bedroom door and laughed. 'You're going soft, Sophie—be careful or you'll become Soft Sophie, Soft Sophie Soft Sophie.'

Sophie pressed her lips hard and counted to ten. 'Don't be stupid, Danny. I don't fall for that anymore. You're the one who ran a mile when you were spooked at the church, just remember that.'

'Goodnight, Sophie.' Danny went to shut the door, and Sophie stopped it with her foot.

'Okay,' she agreed reluctantly. 'You're not going on your own. I don't know why you want to go again. We'll look in the window, but that's it.'

'Whatever, Sophie—I'll be going at midnight, so I'll see you later.'

After synchronising watches, Sophie and Danny agreed to meet them on the landing, with their beds made as before.

Sophie wriggled into her pyjamas while wearing her jeans and T-shirt underneath and sat back in bed. Staring at the ceiling, she remembered her conversation with Mrs Dawson and flinched nervously. Although her alarm was set for five minutes before midnight she lay awake until that time, thoughts twisting and turning in her head. *Who was that boy? And where were his parents? He had to live somewhere—but why was he at the school? And who was the real Mrs Dawson? She was becoming more intriguing with every conversation!*

# CHAPTER 10

hen the time finally came, Sophie and Danny set off for the now familiar backstreets, the night sky gloomily lighting their way. The walk tonight was more solemn, and they spoke very little as they approached the shops.

'It's so quiet back here', Sophie whispered, 'not a soul in sight!'

Sophie immediately felt uneasy. After their previous experiences, she felt the need for other people to be around them, as a sort of security. But who would be around these streets at midnight? She wished they hadn't come, but Danny had been so insistent, and she had been afraid that he would have gone without her. Even with just the two of them, there would be safety in numbers, she thought to herself. She was not reassured.

When they finally reached the backstreet in question, Danny ventured quickly towards the puppet shop window. The other shops no longer held the signs in the windows, but their interiors stayed the same. Sophie wondered if they had been open at all that day. The same orange light dimly lit the puppet shop window, and the puppets hung as before.

Danny pointed. 'Look, it's open!'

The door did seem to be slightly ajar. Sophie felt uneasy, and she shivered at this news.

'Let's go in,' Danny urged. 'I told you it would be worth coming!'

'Danny, it's the middle of the night—there could've been burglars or anything—they might still be in there!'

Danny stepped forward to the doorway, but Sophie stopped him. 'Don't, Danny.'

'Soft Sophie,' he jeered for the second time that evening, his face sneering and unusually cold.

'I'll come with you.' She rolled her shoulders to release a knot of tension embedded in each and placed both hands on the door handle. Something above her caught her eye. Over the door of the shop, a brass sign shone out from the darkness, which read in small etched letters:

*Zauberer*

*Marionette*

Sophie turned the brass handle and pushed hard, as the door scratched open against the floor. 'That's funny,' she whispered as she squeezed through the gap she'd made, 'I don't remember it doing that last time.'

Danny followed, the door swinging open to permit him entry.

They stood together like statues, taking in this strange sight. The shop was lit in the familiar orange, and Sophie noticed, at once, the heavy aroma of wood shavings. As her eyes adjusted to the light, she realised to her horror that they were not alone in the shop. Hunched over the wooden desk, scraping at wood with a dark grey metal tool, was a tall bony figure, old, and shrouded in shadow. His breathing could be heard above the scratching sounds of the carving he was working on, seemingly undisturbed by their arrival. Sophie tried hard to quieten her breathing as it seemed loud and heavy in this small room.

The moment rolled on for what seemed like an eternity, and Sophie stared at the figure, trying to clear her head of chaotic thoughts.

Slowly, the old man looked up. As his face came into the light, she saw that his skin resembled well worn leather. Sunken cheeks revealed sharp cheekbones and a razor thin nose while his mouth twisted tightly downwards into a curved line. From angular shoulders hung a long dark jacket, its colour a midnight blue.

'I am Zauberer' he breathed, without looking up from his work. 'Do sit down.'

The door gently clicked as it closed, Sophie looking quickly to confirm that, yes, they were now locked inside.

Danny followed his instructions immediately without question. He sat cross-legged, and Sophie copied quickly, aware that she wouldn't leave his side. The floor was dusty, and wood shavings curled around their feet.

'You were here before,' he spat, flashing piercing sapphire blue eyes in their direction. Sophie detected an accent but could not place it.

Neither child spoke, but both continued to stare at Mr Zauberer.

Sophie became aware of the moments rolling by and suddenly became very conscious of not speaking.

She opened her mouth and finally blurted, in desperation for something to say, 'We like your puppets. How many do you have?'

'As many as there are stars in the sky,' he breathed, looking up from his desk. His stare was directed, not at her, but towards Danny, and he stared longer than she imagined possible before returning to his work.

'You are so very young,' Zauberer continued, in little more than a whisper. 'You are not from these parts.'

'No, we're from London', she began, forcing herself to engage in conversation that broke the silence, 'and we're here on holiday.'

Mr Zauberer continued his work, seemingly uninterested in her nervous chatter.

'We must get back,' she started, directing these words to Danny. 'Our mums might discover we're gone.'

Danny didn't move; his gaze focused on Mr Zauberer.

'Danny,' Sophie repeated, looking at her watch for effect. He continued to stare, fascinated by what he saw.

'Go, little one,' Mr Zauberer said, motioning to the door. 'You will visit again.'

'Thank you, Mr Zauberer,' Danny said slowly. 'I will visit again.'

He looked up temporarily from his work, his eyes glinting in the half-light as the door clicked open. 'Make sure you do.'

Outside the shop, Sophie and Danny began walking quickly back to the guest house. The sky was starting to show tinges of purples and pinks as dawn crept in. Sophie could feel the tension in her shoulders knot even more tightly as she remembered what had just occurred.

'I thought we were never going to get out of there,' Sophie whispered, when she felt she was far enough away from the shop to speak. As she tried to link arms with Danny, he shrugged her off and continued walking.

'What a scary old man!' she added. 'And working through the night like that. How peculiar!'

Danny frowned. 'He was just busy and had no time to speak with her.'

His voice seemed serious, and Sophie felt it better not to say anything more. Her thoughts were still spinning, making her feel sick and dizzy.

They walked hurriedly in a mutual silence, back to the Sandy Stop Guest House. The door pushed open as before, and while Sophie bolted many locks as quietly as she could, Danny went up to bed without saying goodnight. As she turned to follow him upstairs, she saw a face at the television room door, framed with long silver hair. Sophie gasped before she realised who it was.

'Goodnight, Sophie,' whispered Mrs Dawson, sadly. 'Rest now, my dear.'

Sophie ran upstairs, her head still spinning. The sky was marbling in stripy purples and pinks as she slipped into bed.

Her brief sleep was troubled with wooden puppets blinking at her, their eyes following her around that dark, eerie shop. Mr Zauberer also haunted her dreams, whispering 'Make sure you do.' Over and over again.

# CHAPTER 11

As Sophie opened her eyes the next morning, she watched as the early morning mist changed the sky from purple to pink, to a cloudy sapphire. Looking at her watch, she realised it was still quite early. The digital face of her alarm clock glowed 6.35 *a.m.* She shook the remaining images of troubled dreams out of her head, before tiptoeing down the corridor to Danny and Nina's room.

'Danny,' she whispered as she pushed the door ajar. Inside the room, twin beds sat next to each other, each nesting a curled up Nina and a stretched Danny under their sheets. Nina turned in bed and murmured, disturbed by Sophie's entrance, but soon settled back into her pillow.

Sophie tiptoed to Danny's bed and placed her hand on his shoulder. Her hand squashed down into what she quickly realised were cleverly placed pillows. Danny was not there. Sophie pulled the bedroom door closed behind her and ran downstairs.

From the dawn light ebbing through the curtains of the dining room, Sophie could see that the tables were laid ready for breakfast. No sign of Danny.

Out in the hallway, she stood for a moment and then checked the television room which was also dark and empty. Biting her bottom lip and twisting her hair nervously, she stood, defeated, at the bottom of the staircase, not knowing what to do.

She knew where Danny was heading, but when had he set off back to the puppet shop? Did he sleep at all that night or had he just waited, until she had gone to bed before steeling out alone into the night? As the realisation Danny could be in danger hit her, Sophie gasped, her eyes filling with tears. She shook her head for the second time that morning and wiped her eyes, before unlocking the many brass bolts on the door and stepping outside.

The back doorway opened, and Mrs Dawson walked into the hallway, her silver hair loose around her face and a long, patterned dressing gown pulled tightly around her tiny frame. Sophie looked back nervously, and the old woman returned her glance.

'Sophie.'

'Good morning, Mrs Dawson,' she said, with a tight-lipped smile.

'Where are you going at this time of day? The sun has barely risen.'

Sophie swallowed hard and forced a smile. 'I woke up a bit early. I thought I'd go out for a walk.'

Sophie knew that she wasn't fooling anybody but continued. 'The beach is supposed to be lovely at dawn. I'd better go.'

Mrs Dawson walked over to her. 'Let's sit down, shall we?'

'I can't, Mrs Dawson, I have to go.'

Mrs Dawson reached out for Sophie's hand and gently pulled her back inside. 'What is the matter, little one?'

Sophie wasn't sure how much she dare tell her and remained silent.

'Let's start again, shall we? Come and sit down.'

Sophie followed her into the back room and sat at the wooden table, her heart pounding against her ribcage. She knew she had gone against Mrs Dawson's wishes and was worried about what to say.

'What are your troubles, Sophie?' she started. 'I have never seen you look so frightened.'

'It's Danny. He's not in bed. I have to go and find him.'

Mrs Dawson reached across and took hold of her hand. 'Where is he, Sophie?'

Tears filled the young girl's eyes again, and she brushed them away angrily. 'Probably just watching the sunrise on the beach. I need to go to him.' Sophie stood up and pushed back her chair.

'Zauberer,' Mrs Dawson said quietly.

Shocked at hearing the man's name, Sophie put her hand to her mouth and gasped quietly.

'Zauberer,' Mrs Dawson repeated.

When Sophie answered, she barely whispered. 'Do you know him?'

Mrs Dawson took hold of Sophie's hand again and squeezed it gently. 'I tried to warn you—you were told not to go on the backstreets.'

A tear ran down Sophie's face, and she hung her head as more tears came.

'What's done is done, Sophie. It doesn't matter now. Carry on.'

Sophie covered her face with her hands and sobbed. This all seemed so impossible, and she wasn't even sure why she felt so afraid. Her dreams had remained with her, and with her eyes closed she could see those puppets staring solemnly at her out from the gloom.

Looking at Mrs Dawson again, she could see how sad the old lady looked. How did she know Zauberer? How had she guessed that's where Danny might be? This was perhaps even more serious than even she had thought.

# CHAPTER 12

It was then that Sophie decided to confide in this woman. Events were spiralling out of control, and it was time to act. 'I think he's at the puppet shop. We went last night, and I know that we shouldn't have, but Danny said he'd go on his own, and I didn't want him to. That's where we'd been when we saw you last night.'

'I know.' Mrs Dawson looked troubled for a moment, then motioned for her to continue.

Sophie felt her lip trembling and continued through difficult sobs. 'We met Mr Zauberer there. He was there working on his puppets. He was really creepy, and he frightened me, but Danny didn't get scared.'

'Did he speak to you, Sophie?'

Sophie remembered the conversation and realised that she had not been spoken to. Zauberer had been more interested in Danny from the moment they entered the shop.

'I tried to talk to him, but he just stared at Danny—I've only just realised. I don't even think he even noticed me. Zauberer said to come back but I didn't want to—maybe he never meant for me to go back anyway. It was Danny who wanted to go back.'

Sophie felt fat tears release and roll down her face.

'When you arrived in the village, Sophie, I was afraid something like this may happen.'

'I think Danny has gone back to the shop, Mrs Dawson. What am I going to do?'

Mrs Dawson released a controlled breath and pulled Sophie up with her as she stood. 'We need to work quickly. There is much you need to know.' She collected a selection of glass jars and clay bowls and placed them on an old dressing table at the other side of the room. Placing wire spectacles on her nose, Mrs Dawson began to inspect the jars' contents. Sophie followed the old lady and saw that the jars were filled with many varieties of brightly coloured stones and withered old plants.

'Do you remember our last meeting, Sophie?'

Sophie nodded.

'I spoke to you then about the dangers of the village, about the sadness of this place,' Mrs Dawson sighed. 'I know that I can be honest with you.'

It was then that Sophie realised that there was something very special about Mrs Dawson. Sophie had seen from the moment they had met that she was different. She had tranquillity about her: her way of speaking, moving, and dressing was not only old-fashioned, but almost other-worldly. Sophie paused for a moment, not daring to believe what she was thinking. This was all very strange—maybe she was getting carried away in the moment. Sophie screwed her eyes shut tightly in an attempt to focus on what was important—getting Danny back. If this Mrs Dawson thought she could help, maybe it was worth letting her try.

'You are an intelligent girl with clear vision,' Mrs Dawson said, pulling Sophie back from her thoughts. She smiled and opened a jar containing the same purple stones like the one in her ring.

'Amethyst,' Sophie remembered.

Mrs Dawson nodded. 'You remember I told you that this village has many places of danger. Danny may be in trouble.'

Sophie looked away from the jars. She had felt this too. But what kind of trouble?

'If Zauberer has Danny, we need to be swift,' she said, quickly arranging a selection of the amethyst stones on the dressing table to form a circle. Sophie had thought that the top of the dressing table was glass but on closer inspection, realised that is was mirrored.

'Already, it may be too late. There is only so much that I can do. Sadly, my powers are limited in this situation.'

'What powers?' Sophie frowned.

Mrs Dawson placed two large twinkling stones down on the table. 'I think you are aware of more than you allow yourself to admit. You are not being true to yourself, Sophie. Listen and prepare to open your mind.'

'So you're telling me you're a witch?'

Mrs Dawson continued. 'I harness the powers of nature to do good.'

'This is all too much to take in,' Sophie whispered. 'I don't know if I believe in stuff like this!'

'Just because you choose not to believe does not mean it does not exist. You are learning a very valuable lesson the hard way, my dear.'

'So if you're a white witch, what does that make Mr Zauberer?' Sophie stopped herself from speaking the unspeakable. Could Zauberer really be a dark wizard? The kind she was only familiar with from an older cousin's lead figures and trading cards? She paused as her own thoughts answered the question for her. 'Are you sure, Mrs Dawson?'

Again Mrs Dawson nodded. She took her place in front of the dressing table and rubbed her powder-pink hands together. 'We will talk about this later, Sophie. It is time. Let us see if our fears are true.'

Mrs Dawson placed her hands in the middle of the circle of stones and closed her eyes.

The mirror seemed to marble under her fingers and as she looked into the swirling image, she sighed. Sophie strained to see what

Mrs Dawson saw but could not interpret the shapes in the mirror. Moments passed, and Sophie watched the old woman's face in a bid to understand what was indeed happening. Her normally smooth and welcoming face was frowning, her brow furrowed in concentration. Finally, she looked up and, looking at Sophie, brought herself back into the present.

'Danny is inside the shop,' Mrs Dawson started. 'He is waiting for Zauberer. Zauberer remains in his shop of marionettes and cannot leave that place by his own will. Lead Danny out of the front door. If you can bring Danny away, Zauberer will not follow you. We must try and reach your friend before it is too late.'

Mrs Dawson went to the dining table and sat down.

Sophie followed, asking 'How do you know he won't follow us? Should I call the police? Wouldn't that make more sense?'

Mrs Dawson shook her head and waited. 'We must act quickly. Zauberer will not be stopped by such trinkets.'

'What did you . . . see?' Sophie asked in hushed tones, not daring to believe her own ears. 'In the mirror—could you see Danny there?'

'You will need to go to Danny and bring him back,' Mrs Dawson answered, neglecting to explain the mystery unfolding. 'This child is in danger. Only you can save him.'

Sophie placed her hands together tightly in her lap and focused intently on a small spider scurrying across the wooden floorboards. As her head cleared, she looked up and nodded.

Mrs Dawson smiled warmly, and Sophie felt a flicker of bravery inside her; she could—she would—do this.

'Take these stones,' Mrs Dawson started, pressing cold misshapen marbles into her hand. 'Amber will encourage you to do what is necessary, and this amethyst will help you to see your situation more clearly.' She spoke slowly and seriously as she held the orange and purple stones up into the light. Sophie recognised the amethyst, her favourite stone.

The old lady held out a burgundy velvet bag, and Sophie tipped the stones into it. Its gold drawstrings were pulled tight before the bag was pressed into Sophie's hand.

Mrs Dawson continued, 'You must go back to the shop and find Danny. Do not go anywhere but the main shop. Do not go down the staircase or towards the back of the shop. You must not approach Zauberer. If Danny is there, pull him out of the shop and run back here with him. Bring him to me, and I will do the rest.' She spoke slowly, with ceremony, and Sophie felt the rhythm of her words.

'Will you come with me?' Sophie asked. 'I can't go there on my own.'

'I can't, my dear. You know so little about my past,' she started. 'There have been many times when I have faced similar troubles. Long ago, when I was much younger, the puppet shop was a place I crept to one night. Zauberer knows me well, and my presence could cause more harm to Danny. Take these stones, and keep them close. They will protect you on your journey.'

Sophie placed the bag of amber and amethyst in her jacket pocket. Mrs Dawson placed two silver cords around Sophie's neck. Each held a smooth round pebble with a hole in its centre threaded onto it. 'When you are close enough to Danny, place one of these around his neck. Each charm will protect you.'

She touched them and looked again at the old lady. 'I don't understand. Will I be safe?'

'You are a special child, Sophie. I knew that when I first met you. Your name itself means truth. These charms can help you if you trust them. But look to your heart to find your own strength. These stones will not save you. They are there to help you. Please don't be blind to the troubles you face. Go now, before the world awakes.' She reached out and grabbed Sophie's arm as she stood up to leave. 'I will be with you, my dear, and nearby if I sense danger,' she whispered before letting go.

# Chapter 13

Sophie half walked, half ran to the backstreet where she and Danny had spent the previous afternoon. Her heart pounded against her ribcage as she resisted the urge to slow down for breath. Her thoughts drummed against her skull as she ran over the cobblestones towards the puppet shop.

As Sophie approached the shop, she saw Danny inside talking with Mr Zauberer. She stood silently in the shadows, watching carefully. They seemed deep in conversation. She saw that Danny held a puppet in his arms. Mr Zauberer was obviously discussing how he had made it as he pointed at joints and pulled at strings. Danny seemed very interested and lacking in any of the terror the pair of them had felt in that shop the day before. She watched as Danny sat down on Zauberer's work table. Taking a miniature bottle carefully from a small tapestry bag, Mr Zauberer unscrewed the bottle's lid and picked up a tall elegant-looking glass. Sophie watched, in what seemed like slow motion, as he poured a shiny yellow liquid until the glass was half full. Gasping, she realised who the drink was for and watched helplessly as Danny reached out for the glass.

As quickly as she could, although her whole body felt stiff and heavy, Sophie ran over to the shop door and turned the handle. The door seemed stiff again, and she pushed with all her strength. Rattling the door as panic washed over her, she realised it would not open.

With both hands curled into tight fists, she started to gently knock on the glass of the door, so as not to alert Mr Zauberer. Neither he nor Danny reacted. Sophie began knocking louder and louder, but still neither of them acknowledged her presence. As Mr Zauberer handed Danny the glass, Sophie banged as loudly as she could on the glass.

'Danny! Danny!' she screamed, over and over again, realising that something was horribly wrong. 'Why can't you hear me? Why can't you hear me?' she sobbed as she continually banged on the glass.

In front of her very eyes, Danny drank the contents of the glass and turned towards the door. He didn't seem to see her as he then turned and walked off down the staircase. Sophie continued banging on the door, until Danny had disappeared from view. As she stood in silence, not sure what she had just witnessed, Mr Zauberer turned and stared at her, his mouth curled in a satisfied sneer, before following Danny downstairs. Sophie watched, helplessly, until Danny was gone.

A seagull called out from a nearby rooftop, and Sophie jumped. She didn't know how long she had been stood outside the puppet shop. Her mind flooded with what she had just seen, and her heart tightened.

She looked desperately inside the shop past the solemn faces of the many puppets hanging in the window. Their eyes stared out at her, as they had so many times in her dreams, while she searched in vain for Mr Zauberer or Danny. Emptying the velvet bag into her hand, she eyed the stones angrily. 'You were a great help,' she whispered harshly as she threw them away down the street. Sophie turned and walked quickly back to the guest house, angry and afraid of what was yet to come.

# CHAPTER 11

s Sophie entered the dining room, her unsteady breathing seemed to fill the place. Mrs Dawson turned towards her, her arms full of empty plates and cutlery.

'Sophie.'

At this, Sophie burst into tears and ran over to Mrs Dawson. 'Danny couldn't hear me. I shouted and banged on the door, the window, but he didn't hear me. Mr Zauberer saw me and took Danny downstairs.'

'Zauberer's strength is renewed. I hoped this would never happen again.'

Sophie sat down at a table and buried her head in her hands. 'I really don't understand, Mrs Dawson. What's happening?'

Her soft hands rested gently on Sophie's head. 'These are troubled times. There are forces of evil at work here, and we need to be swift to overcome them.'

'Again?'

'Zauberer was the cause of much heartache in the past. Many have perished under his powers. We have one hour before breakfast. Follow me.' And with that, Mrs Dawson rushed away down the corridor. Sophie ran after her, wiping away her tears.

In the apartment that Sophie had visited earlier that morning, Mrs Dawson busied herself collecting jars and books from the shelves and cupboard tops around the main room where they were sat. Sophie sat down at the now familiar wooden table and watched her mind a jumble of the reality and dreams that had lived with her over the last few days and nights. A blur of fantasy and reality, she struggled to understand where she stood in all of this and what part she could possibly play.

'The first thing we must do is take care that your mother and aunt know nothing of Danny's disappearance. Children are more difficult to hide the truth from, but adults allow their minds to be clouded so easily.' Mrs Dawson picked up a large dusty brown book from the table. 'Now then, just a temporary mist I think.'

'What are you going to do to them?' Sophie asked as she moved to look more closely at the page Mrs Dawson was squinting at.

'All natural ingredients, my dear.' She smiled, patting Sophie's arm. 'Remember I am working with the good magics of the natural world, not the evil sorcery of Zauberer's kind.'

Sophie watched as the steady crinkled fingers flicked through page after page of ancient, handwritten notes.

'Here we are!' she exclaimed as she leaned further forward as if to inhale the recipe from the page. 'A sweet tea made from rosewood and clary sage, with a sprinkling of petals from the forget-me-not flower. This will relax and mist the mind so they will be sure that Danny is safe and nearby, just like Nina.'

'It won't hurt them, will it?'

Mrs Dawson laughed. 'My dear! There are people who pay good money for such remedies! This simply allows us to work without disturbance. Fear not. I will serve the tea to your mother and aunt at breakfast, and they will be blissfully unaware of Danny's absence for a time. Leave me to work, and join your family at the breakfast table at eight o'clock. Leave a seat for Danny as usual, and I will do the rest. Go my child!'

Sophie ran quietly upstairs and sat at the end of her bed. Her watch glowed 6.45 *a.m.*, and Sophie realised she had not slept for more than two hours that night. Her body felt strangely awake, and her mind was clear. Sophie looked down at the rose and lilac covered archway. The little boy was sat underneath, looking up at Sophie's window. When he saw Sophie he jumped up and hid behind it, peeping out at Sophie between the twisted climbing branches.

Sophie opened her window and whispered down as loudly as she dare. 'Hey! Don't be frightened! I'm a friend of Mrs Dawson!'

The boy peeped out. 'Come down to the garden,' he called. 'I'll be here.'

Sophie looked at her watch. 6.59 *a.m.* She waved in agreement and then ran silently downstairs.

The door was quickly unbolted, and Sophie tiptoed through a tall ivy-covered passageway into the back-garden. She had forgotten her sneakers, and her bare toes flexed as they sank into the dewy grass. Trees and bushes grew thick and green in the garden. In every spare border sat clusters of pink-and-blue flowers.

'Hello,' Sophie whispered.

'Good morning,' the boy replied.

A robin hopped across the lawn between the two children, and they watched as it tugged out a worm from the opposite border. Sophie walked quickly to meet the boy, and they stood together in silence by the sweet scented arch. On closer inspection, she realised that he was indeed the boy from the school. His dirty brown hair still flopped over his face as before, and his hazel eyes, although less frightened this time, were still as wide as ever.

'My name is Lawrence,' he continued. 'And you're Sophie.'

'Yes,' Sophie replied, frowning. 'How do you know my name?'

'Holly told me,' he began. 'She has told me of your family.'

The penny dropped, and Sophie smiled in relief. 'Holly is Mrs Dawson?'

The boy nodded and looked back to the robin. It had gone.

'I saw you at the village school,' Sophie continued nervously. 'I'm sorry I ran away but my friend got scared.'

The two sat down on the carpet of lilac and rose confetti and picked at the petals.

'I love this garden,' Lawrence murmured.

'Why do you come here? I've seen you visit Mrs Dawson from my window.'

Lawrence rubbed blades of grass through his fingers. 'Holly looks after me. She is all I have.'

'She told me your parents are gone. I'm sorry.'

'My life could be a lot worse,' Lawrence whispered, without looking up. 'Holly saved me.'

'From what?' Sophie asked, desperate for some answers.

Lawrence finally met Sophie's gaze. 'Where is the other boy?'

'Danny?' Sophie squeezed her hands together, unsure what she could say. 'Mrs Dawson is helping me find him.'

The two watched each other curiously then looked over to the house. Mrs Dawson was stood in the doorway.

'Good morning!' she called. The two children looked uneasily at each other, their meeting now discovered.

'Run along, Sophie,' she ordered, with a smile that reassured Sophie they weren't in any trouble. 'You and Lawrence will meet again this afternoon. We will need his help.'

Sophie smiled timidly at Lawrence and ran back to the house to prepare herself for breakfast.

# CHAPTER 15

When Sophie finally came down for breakfast that morning, her mum, Auntie Penny and Nina were already there. Sophie left a space for Danny, as Mrs Dawson had told her, and sat next to Nina.

'Is he still sleeping?' Auntie Penny asked as Sophie settled in her chair.

'I didn't like to wake him,' Sophie lied, looking at Nina for a flicker of suspicion. Nina didn't flinch.

Sophie watched Mrs Dawson approach the table, hardly daring to breathe.

'Cup of tea?' she asked politely in her usual way.

'Ooh, lovely,' the two aunties replied together.

Mrs Dawson smiled and poured the tea, filling the china cups with clear dark orange liquid.

Sophie's mum added milk and took a slurp. She looked up at Mrs Dawson. 'This is very refreshing—but not the usual tea you serve.'

Sophie looked up, startled.

'I thought I'd try a different brand,' Mrs Dawson replied. 'What do you think?'

'Lovely,' Auntie Penny replied, taking a few sips and then replacing her cup carefully in her saucer.

Breakfast passed by in the usual way, and the conversation moved seamlessly between plans for a day on the beach, weather forecasts, and predictions for lunch and dinner. Sophie breathed uneasily through pursed lips, waiting for Danny's absence to be commented on. As the last of the tea was slurped and sipped, Mrs Dawson came to their table.

'Everything all right for you this morning?' she asked, in her usual way.

'As always!' Sophie's mum replied. 'We're ready for anything now. Well, anything that sunbathing on a beach all day might throw at us!'

'Where's Danny?' Nina asked suddenly. 'He's not had his breakfast.'

'He'll have it when he wakes up.' Auntie Penny laughed. 'Are you all set for the beach, Sophie?'

Sophie screwed up her nose at the thought.

'I wonder if I could be so bold,' Mrs Dawson interrupted. 'I spoke to Sophie about her artistic talents earlier this week. She offered to paint a new house sign for my gatepost.'

'Could I do it today?' Sophie pleaded. 'I really can't bear another day at the beach!'

'I suppose Danny will want to stay, too,' Auntie Penny added.

'As long as you don't mind, Mrs Dawson.' Sophie's mum smiled.

'Not at all,' the landlady replied. 'Sophie's doing *me* the favour.'

With that the family went upstairs to prepare for their day at the beach.

Once inside her room, Sophie realised that the tea must have worked instantly. They hadn't forgotten Danny, they just hadn't realised he wasn't around.

When Mum, Auntie Penny, and Nina, had left for the beach, Sophie made her bed and glanced out of the window for a moment. There was no sign of Lawrence. As soon as she was sure breakfast was over and the other guests would be gone, she ran downstairs to the kitchen door. After knocking lightly, Mrs Dawson let her in and led her to the back room. Sophie was surprised to see Lawrence already sat at the table.

'Sit down,' he said. 'We have so much to discuss.'

Sophie frowned. She wanted to be polite but wasn't sure she wanted to be ordered around by someone not much older than her. She remained standing and waited for Mrs Dawson to speak.

After sitting down herself, Mrs Dawson motioned to the empty chair, and Sophie obeyed, a little cross at her own stubbornness.

'You are an intelligent girl with an open mind, Sophie,' Mrs Dawson began. 'Lawrence and I will tell you many things that you will find difficult.'

Around the table, the three sighed collectively, then smiled. The ice broken, Sophie relaxed and warmed to Lawrence once more.

# CHAPTER 16

'My life has been a troubled one,' Lawrence began, shifting awkwardly in his seat. 'Holly is the only one who has shared it with me.'

Sophie frowned at Mrs Dawson. 'I don't understand what this has to do with Danny.'

'This has everything to do with Danny,' Mrs Dawson replied. 'Lawrence's troubles also started with an innocent visit to Zauberer's puppet shop.'

Lawrence put his hands to his mouth as if he were about to cry. 'Like so many others,' he muttered sadly through his fingers.

'Zauberer is a dangerous individual. He is not of this world.' Mrs Dawson stopped and placed her hand over Sophie's. 'He began his crusade many years ago.'

'Crusade?' echoed Sophie.

'To steal the power of childhood, wherever he may be.'

Sophie's eyes widened, not daring to believe what was being said.

Mrs Dawson continued. 'Over many years he has travelled the world, stopping in towns and villages where he saw an abundance of children. Germany, Australia, India, China, it didn't matter where. He would settle into the local community with his collection of puppets and then before too long, children would start to disappear.'

Lawrence interrupted. 'Only one at first, then a couple more, then more and more until there would be fear and dread in the hearts of all who lived in that village. When he felt his task was complete, he would pack up and move on.'

'His task was only ever complete when the children of the village were all gone,', Mrs Dawson explained.

'But where did the children go?' Sophie asked.

'Zauberer is very a powerful sorcerer,' Mrs Dawson continued. 'His powers increased every time a child 'disappeared'. When he came to our seaside village, we were unaware of what a danger he was. It was only when poor Lawrence was threatened that I discovered what was happening.'

Lawrence rubbed his hands painfully, as if preparing himself for what he was about to say. 'My dear friends, Amy and Clara, had told me about the magic of the puppet shop before they disappeared.'

'Your friends disappeared too?' Sophie gasped.

'Yes. I had been heartbroken and had started wandering away from school and home each evening without warning anyone of where I was going. One evening, I met Zauberer and was enchanted by his stories of the beautiful countries I had never seen. I too wanted to travel. I was to visit him on two more occasions to talk of the ocean and far off lands.' He swallowed hard and looked at Mrs Dawson. She nodded for him to continue. 'It was on the third visit that I fell into his grasp. He had offered me a drink in an ornate crystal glass. I had taken the thick amber juice down in one swift gulp. The next I knew, I awoke among the wood shavings of the shop's cellar floor in pitch darkness.'

'Danny drank the juice,' Sophie interrupted. 'What do we do now?'

'Patience, Sophie,' whispered Mrs Dawson. 'There is much more you need to know.'

Lawrence went on. 'I felt confused and afraid. Zauberer revived me, offering a second draught of the liquid, which I drank, being led to believe that it would wake me from my faint. My body tightened and buckled. I heard sickening screams then realised they were my own. The pain was unimaginable.'

Sophie gasped. 'Danny was taken downstairs. Oh no—he drank from the glass! What will Zauberer do to him?'

Without acknowledging Sophie's words, as if now transported back in time to his own meeting with Zauberer, Lawrence continued his story. 'My sister had always told me that if I was ever in trouble, I should call out to her silently, using my thoughts. I had never known her true powers.'

At this, Sophie, frowned in confusion. 'Your sister?'

'I am his sister, Sophie,' Mrs Dawson spoke gently. 'My powers were much stronger then and I could hear Lawrence's screams as I walked home from school that evening. I had been teaching for a short time and was distressed by the steady disappearance of children from the village. Two dear sisters called Amy and Clara, friends of our family, were missing too, and this had been hard for us all. As I walked, I could hear Lawrence's cries and so, I followed the sounds through the backstreets. Once inside the shop, I saw Zauberer for the first time. I had sensed danger in the village but was unaware of this shop and Zauberer himself. I walked into the shop and sensed evil immediately. It overpowered me, and I remember realising what danger we were all in. The walls were filled with the familiar faces of children I had taught, and in the window, I saw Amy and Clara resting against each other in the matching dresses they loved to wear. The change in them was painful—now in miniature, their bodies twisted into awkward positions, strung up imprisoned by silver wires and nailed to the wall.'

Sophie gasped as the true horror of what was happening unfolded. 'I've seen them; they're still in the window!'

Mrs Dawson squeezed Sophie's shoulder and continued. 'In those days, I had the ability to cast many different spells. As I raised my hand to start my magic, Zauberer realised his danger and set evil forces against me.'

Sophie imagined the scene as Mrs Dawson spoke of a battle where coloured lights and mists filled the workshop. Her words flooded over her as she spoke of calling the powers of Mother Earth. Flying images of spiders and toads, cats and red-breasted robins flashed in front of her before she heard the silence and focused again on Mrs Dawson.

'The power of Zauberer was too great. Exhausted, I called on the magic of the Earth to help me. While Zauberer fell to the floor, I ran to the cellar where my little brother lay, contorted and lifeless. Thinking he was dead, I fled from the shop with him in my arms. Before I left I called a final enchantment, a curse above the door of the shop. Zauberer was doomed to spend eternity inside there, trapped away from the other children of the world.'

'Wow,' Sophie whispered. 'That is unreal.'

'No, Sophie,' Lawrence sighed. 'Sadly, that was very real. So many children lost, so many souls trapped. Zauberer's evil stole so many—I cannot bear to think of it.'

# CHAPTER 17

This unlikely team sat in silence, the ticking wall clock the only sound to be heard as the reality of the situation sank in.

'If only we had known he could still entice children into his workshop,' Lawrence muttered. 'If only we'd known. How many more . . .'

'We cannot think of those things. I have watched carefully over the years, few children ever come here. I cannot imagine there being others before Danny, my dear brother. Try not to trouble yourself further.'

Lawrence sat quietly, his eyes downward, his hands tightly knotted in his lap. Sophie swallowed with difficulty before speaking again. 'But, your magic, is it all gone?'

'As I have told you before,' Mrs Dawson sighed, 'I have been left with limited powers. It is important to strengthen them by working with the powers of nature. They will help us to fight this evil.'

'Holly saved my life.' Lawrence smiled. 'However, I had drunk one glass of the potion, and my body changed painfully over one night. If I had drunk another glass, my soul would have been stolen from me, my body fully contorted and shrunken into a tiny wooden figure. The puppets are stolen children, Sophie, their souls drained from them to enrich Zauberer's power. After that one night, as I experienced an agony I had never before imagined possible, my skin took on this strange quality. My heart is frozen in time, my skin the appearance of wood. I have lived for seventy years, but my body is that of a twelve years old boy.'

Sophie gasped again, now embarrassed about how annoyed she had felt towards Lawrence earlier that day.

'We need to be swift,' Mrs Dawson said finally. 'You will need to go alone but with the powers of nature to help you. Tomorrow is Friday. It is the day of the week when forces of nature are at their strongest. We must wait until then. You will go to Zauberer and distract him; take him to the cellar to admire his carvings. Once you have led him out of the way, we shall prepare the shop in our bid to destroy him once and for all!'

Sophie frowned, her head throbbing as she tried to take this all in. 'But why can't you go? Surely it would be better for you and safer if I stayed away—what can I do?'

Mrs Dawson patted her hand. 'Zauberer knows me—Danny will be safer if we prepare the workshop with Zauberer out of the way. We will be but moments away. With you in spirit and near enough to step in should we need to.'

'The day is almost over,' Lawrence added, looking out of the window as the summer sun faded.

Sophie looked at her watch. It read 5.46 p.m. 'Can't we go now?'

Mrs Dawson reached for Sophie's hand and held it tightly. 'Since my last encounter, I have needed to work with the powers of nature, not against them. You must learn to do the same.'

Sophie slumped forward and sobbed, anxiously.

'I know it is difficult, my dear, but we must wait for the right moment. Zauberer is a powerful creature. We will exhaust every inch of our beings in our attempt to overthrow him.'

Sophie nodded and stood up. 'What time should I be here?'

'Tomorrow morning, we will start early. Come to us at six o'clock, and we will prepare you for the most important day you will ever have to face.'

Sophie left the room and closed the door, not once looking behind her. The twilight of the early evening made her feel lost between two worlds, and she wished for a moment to be back home with her friends, before any of this had ever happened.

# Chapter 18

Sophie blinked sleepily as her eyes opened to the faint bleeping of her alarm. She turned to her watch, which glowed blearily 5.55 *a.m.* out of the darkness.

Once downstairs, she knocked quietly at the kitchen door and was let in by Lawrence without a sound.

As she walked into the room, she saw many items laid out in preparation around her. On the wooden table were laid many coloured stones and strangely shaped objects in neat rows. Sophie sat down as she rubbed her eyes and waited for Mrs Dawson to speak.

'In front of you are many special things,' Mrs Dawson started. 'These will safeguard you from harm while you visit Zauberer. Let me give you a new red velvet purse in which to place your charms.'

Sophie blushed as she remembered what she had done with the last one.

'Here is a branch from the rowan tree—this will protect you on your journey. Keep it safe. And here is a strip of snakeskin. It is an ancient charm. Place it over the door of the puppet shop before you enter, and it will protect all inside the building from harm.' Mrs Dawson slipped in the branch, the length of Sophie's index finger into the bag followed by a dull grey piece of leather, a little like a small bookmark. Holding up a handful of soft yellow petals for Sophie to smell, she continued. 'Once inside, throw these jasmine petals on the floor to relax Zauberer

and make him feel sleepy. He will offer you the crystal glass as you have visited him two times before. Take the potion from him, but ask to see the cellar.'

As Sophie breathed in the sweet perfume of the petals in Mrs Dawson's hand, she looked up in to the old woman's eyes.

'What do I do then? He will expect me to drink the potion, surely?'

'Trust the petals. He will be off guard at this point and will prepare to guide you down the stairs at this point, as he has done so many times before. You will make it easy for him and in his eagerness to take you to the cellar he will be distracted from the potion. As he turns to descend the cellar stairs, pour away the liquid.'

Lawrence interrupted. 'It is as thick as treacle, so you may have to assist it and scrape it out with a handkerchief or such like.'

'I'll take one with me,' Sophie decided.

Mrs Dawson handed her a white cotton handkerchief delicately embroidered with flowers along one length. 'Put this in your pocket now, should you need it.'

Collecting some stones from their glass jars, she continued. 'Sophie, you must then let him take you to the cellar. Find your courage here, my dear. I know you will feel afraid. But once you are downstairs, Lawrence and I will enter the shop and prepare for our revenge. I give you now another piece of amber and amethyst as you rejected the others in anger.' The orange and purple stones felt cold and smooth in Sophie's hand as they chinked gently together. She stroked them lightly before dropping them in the velvet bag Mrs Dawson held open.

'You must also wear this.' She handed Sophie a brooch in the shape of a snake with a long forked tongue twisting from its mouth. 'This will protect you from Zauberer's evil stare which has hypnotised so many before you.'

As Sophie dropped the brooch in the velvet bag, Mrs Dawson asked, 'Do you have your pendant?'

Smiling nervously, Sophie pulled out the rounded pebble threaded on a silver string from under her clothing.

'Take care to wear it at all times,' Lawrence urged.

'After breakfast, we will continue the day as normal. You will spend the day with your family, and I will continue here as usual. We must not allow any suggestion of what we will do to slip. Zauberer will know if we plot and plan for too long. He will sense that something is wrong. After dinner we will wait until as late as possible.'

'It has to be before midnight,' Lawrence interrupted. 'This has to be done on Friday, the powers of nature are with us more strongly then.'

'So, that's decided.' Mrs Dawson stood up and walked to the door. 'Meet us tonight at eleven o'clock. We will then go to Zauberer.'

The day dragged by, and Sophie thought it would never end. After a lazy walk around the arcades with Nina, she sat beside her on a bench overlooking the ocean. As Nina slurped on a pink foot-shaped ice-lolly, Sophie followed the pathways of various seagulls as they looped across the sky.

'Where's Danny?' Nina asked.

'He's around,' Sophie answered, looking ahead of her without blinking.

'Something's going on.'

Sophie waited until the seagull she was following flew out of view. 'Trust me Nina, he's around.'

'I'm scared.'

Sophie put her arm around Nina's shoulders and gave her a slight squeeze. 'Trust me Nina. You'll see him really soon.'

Nina read the joke silently on her lolly stick before glancing up at Sophie, her eyes narrow and questioning. 'I do trust you. But things are just a bit weird.'

Sophie smiled and stood up. 'Come on. Our mums will be waiting for us.'

They ran down to the sand and shared apple sandwiches—Nina's favourite—before working on a monster sandcastle together for most of the afternoon. After digging out a moat, Nina got to work making turrets and doorways, while Sophie collected seashells in pinks and creams to decorate the walls. Sophie was aware that she should keep busy so that Zauberer would suspect nothing. A bridge across the moat was sculpted in the style of an open drawbridge, and it was almost complete.

'I know,' Nina started digging into her pocket. 'Let's make a flag.'

Sophie waved her lolly stick and looked around for a flag.

'Here,' Auntie Penny called, waving a paper napkin. 'Will this do?'

Sophie worked swiftly, folding and wrapping the red napkin around the stick, securing it with one of her hair grips. Finally, it was complete.

'Perfect!' Nina shouted. 'Let's take a photo!'

Sophie photographed Nina with the castle, the castle alone, Nina in the moat, and so on until her camera film whirred to a grizzly end.

The walk home, even though they were laden down with sandy bags and towels was, for the first time, almost enjoyable for Sophie. She felt the tight knot in her chest almost leave her as Nina skipped along by her side, chatting endlessly about the sandcastle and the photos.

Sitting with Nina that evening, in front of the television, the two girls enjoyed laughing at the dated clothes the characters were wearing in re-runs of ancient sitcoms.

'Off to bed, Nina, you need your beauty sleep,' Auntie Penny called from the settee. 'Tomorrow will be a big day, with all the packing and travelling home.'

Nina groaned and stood up.

'I think I'll go too,' Sophie said, pretending to yawn. 'I'm worn out.'

Sophie's mum and Auntie Penny raised their eyebrows at each other and laughed. 'Well off you go then sleepy head!'

Sophie and Nina were soon at the top of the stairs outside Sophie's bedroom door.

'Goodnight, Nina, sleep well.'

'Is Danny here?'

'Don't worry—he'll be fine. Try not to worry.'

'So I'll see him tomorrow, will I?'

Sophie opened her door and pretended to yawn one more time. 'Of course. Sweet dreams.' Sophie entered the darkness of her room and closed the door.

# CHAPTER 19

Time crawled as Sophie lay wide awake beneath her bed sheets. As she watched her clock flash through the darkness, minute by minute towards eleven o'clock, her head swam with the strange events of the last few days.

Finally, Sophie could bear it no longer. She pulled on her navy blue parka over a woollen jumper and dark denim jeans, worn in the hope that she would melt into the night sky, later running to Zauberer's shop. Her silver snake brooch nestled itself in the wool of her jumper. Its presence gave her no real feeling of protection, just an unnerving pressure of what may occur over the next few hours. Ten minutes before she was expected, she zipped up her jacket and tiptoed downstairs to meet Mrs Dawson in the hallway.

'Do you have all I gave you, Sophie?'

Sophie pulled out the velvet pouch and held it up.

'Do exactly as we told you. You will need to work with the charms I have shown you and believe in them.' Holding Sophie's face, she spoke once more. 'Without them you will be powerless.'

Sophie and Mrs Dawson stood silently, their hands clasped together, willing the other to be strong.

As Sophie left the house, shutting the door behind her, the starless night and a crisp breeze followed her as she ran through the winding streets towards the puppet shop.

Yellow light ebbed from the familiar window, and Sophie paused before entering. She fumbled for the leathery snake skin in her bag and placed it carefully above her on the top of the door frame. With care, she pushed the door gently open and slipped silently inside. Breathing in the smell of sawdust, her eyes flickered across faces of the puppet children hanging painfully from the walls. She tried quickly to take in her surroundings, nervous of being here alone, aware of her heart beating heavily against her ribs. Suddenly, her eyes fell on the carved bottle and ornate drinking glass high on a shelf behind Zauberer's work table.

A noise broke Sophie's concentration, and she turned to the stone archway. Creak followed creak as Zauberer trod heavily up the stairs.

Sophie felt her breath twist in her throat and she touched the velvet bag in her pocket for reassurance. Rubbing the small rowan twig that lay with the other charms, she remembered what Mrs Dawson had told her. *It will protect you on your journey.* Now Sophie didn't feel quite so alone with these hidden charms shrouded in velvet. She had felt powerless against the events that were about to unfold and was unsure that these charms could do anything to keep her safe. This seemed so fantastical, like a dusty library book opening to reveal a fairy tale from long ago, one that she was being led to believe in, to put her trust in. She just wasn't sure. This all seemed such a bad idea.

'Good evening, Sophie,' a voice crackled from the stone archway.

Sophie jumped, jarred from her thoughts. It had begun.

'Good evening, Mr Zauberer,' Sophie whispered, forcing her voice to sound calm and quiet.

He left the shadows and stood by his work table. 'I have been expecting you.'

'I—I thought—' Sophie panicked and words left her for a moment.

'You thought you would visit me and my children.' He peered forward at the silver snake brooch pinned on Sophie's jumper, and she touched it, reassured when her fingers met the cold metal.

'Yes,' Sophie said, blinking back frightened tears.

'Why don't we sit down? You must have many questions.' He sat in his work seat and gestured to a nearby stool. Sophie sat and knotted her fingers in her lap.

'Where's Danny?' Sophie gasped and brought her hand to her mouth quickly as she realised what she had said. The darkness of the room and the scent of wood shavings made her feel drowsy, and she had been caught off guard.

'You came for Danny,' Zauberer smiled, gently. He didn't seem as terrifying in this light, his face softer, his voice whispering. Sophie could sense a calm covering her, almost like a soft, warm blanket. Sophie relaxed.

'Danny came here, and I came to find him,' she nodded. The room seemed to throb in alternating ruby and amber, yet Sophie found this comforting and sat back on the stool, her hands relaxed in her lap. The bag of charms sat in her pocket but lay there undetected, unused, as Sophie sat in conversation with this strange man.

'Danny will join my children as you too may wish to.'

Zauberer had answered her earlier question, admitting his plans, but Sophie felt no danger, no concern. The words washed over her, and although she heard them, they did not concern her. The room echoed his words, until she almost heard musical whispers, gentle reassurances from the mouths of the puppets on the walls.

Sophie heard her voice but couldn't control it. 'The puppets are beautiful,' she whispered. 'It would be an honour to be part of this family.'

Zauberer busied himself, collecting bottles and glasses from a shelf behind him as Sophie looked at the hands in her lap. They were joined together, her palms creating a small bowl as she had done when she had accepted her first Holy Communion wafer a few years earlier. As she looked closely, she saw a tiny yellow jasmine petal sitting in the centre of her upturned palm, and she instinctively brought it up to her nose and breathed in deeply.

The fog cleared. She looked up and caught the old man staring at her, intently, and with that Sophie jerked back into the present. Her eyes scanned the room, and she saw the children hanging there, their eyes looking out sorrowfully as they waited for her to join them. Sophie had come so close, she realised, to meet a similar fate as these poor unfortunate souls around her. How many times had he lured a child into this room, and how often had some poor innocent been drugged with the scent of sandalwood, the ebb and flow of the room's soft lights until they too had heard their mouth whisper the acceptance of this cruel and futile end?

# Chapter 20

She would have to work quickly. Without a sound, she reached into the depths of her velvet purse. The amber and amethyst rubbed against her fingers, and she felt strangely warmed by the simple knowledge that they were there. She pulled out the silky jasmine petals and scattered them around her chair. They fell around her as Zauberer turned back to continue his game. After placing the amber bottle and glass on the table in front of her, he pulled up a chair and sat down.

'How do you make the puppets?' Sophie spoke quickly, words tumbling from her mouth in a bid to stay safe and out of danger.

Zauberer frowned. 'Now Sophie. You know better.'

He stood and turned reaching up to the shelf where the bottle and glass sat. 'This is what you came for.' Sophie gasped and moved back on her stool.

'You watched Danny. Now it's your turn.' Zauberer shuddered and looked at her sharply, his eyes blue and piercing. 'I knew you would be back. Do you think you can save him?'

'No,' Sophie mouthed.

'You are only a girl, Sophie. A pawn in my game of chess. Nothing more.'

He walked over, pouring the last of the bottle's sticky amber substance into the glass, before placing it into Sophie's hand. He then sat, wearily, back in his chair. Sophie glanced down at the jasmine petals beneath him and breathed in sharply, waiting and hoping, daring to believe in Mrs Dawson's magic now and willing it to do as she wished.

Zauberer motioned with a flick of his bony wrist, before leaning heavily against the table.

Sophie's mind cleared suddenly as she felt the coldness of the drink through the crystal. It may take time, she thought, for the petals to relax him. How long would it take? Sophie held the glass tightly.

'Do I have to—?'

'Drink.' Zauberer tapped the glass sharply as he said this, his eyes heavy.

Sophie remembered Mrs Dawson's instructions and realised that she must keep him in that chair so the jasmine petals would relax him. 'Do I have to go downstairs?'

The old man frowned suspiciously.

Sophie felt tears again. She rubbed her eyes dry. 'I saw Danny. Do I have to go too?'

'But of course. It's your—how shall I say—your destiny.'

He leaned over and tried to take the glass from her. His movement was clumsy but determined, and Sophie panicked. She jumped up and began walking back towards the stairs.

'Drink.'

Zauberer stood and blocked her way. It was only now that Sophie realised how tall and strong he really was. The glass in her hand was the only thing between them. He had moved away from the chair, and the jasmine petals lay helplessly strewn beyond them both. Sophie was sure she would have to drink the liquid. The petals had failed. As he stood in front of her now, she started to cry.

'Drink.' His cruel smile carved on twisted lips betrayed the softness of his voice as he pushed her back, back, back, until she was trapped against the wall.

In his height, his strength and power had returned. Towering over her now, Zauberer pushed the glass violently to her lips, and she felt her bottom lip bruise against her teeth as the thick glass pressed against them.

'Drink!' he shouted. She tightened her lips together as the bitter thickness of the potion stung her mouth. She panicked and pushed the glass away. It fell, smashing, amber droplets scattering like jewels across the floor.

Zauberer grabbed Sophie by the hair and pulled her to him. 'Downstairs,' he growled and pulled her after him as she stumbled down the staircase, struggling to stay on her feet.

Once downstairs, he threw her away from him, and she fell backwards into a corner. Dazed, for a moment, she lay twisted, before curling herself up into a tight shell, in a vain attempt to protect herself from him. Her amethyst and amber pressed painfully into her as they lay hidden in her pocket, and she carefully pulled the bag out into her hand. Their presence was now her only hope, and even though it all felt so hopeless now, she clutched them tightly, willing them to be much more than a collection of lucky charms.

Zauberer opened a small wooden chest to reveal further bottles of the liquid she had seen drain from the bottle upstairs. He pulled one out and reached in for a matching crystal goblet like the one now smashed upstairs.

'Look, little one, I have more.' He poured a new measure and held it in front of her. 'You will drink now.'

Sophie put one hand over her mouth, but he roughly dragged it away. In the chaos, her velvet bag fell to the floor and emptied its secrets at Zauberer's feet.

Distracted for a moment, he kicked them away from him and smiled.

'Sophie, Sophie, Sophie,' he whispered, stepping closer and closer, with each breath. 'Trinkets will not protect you. You are mine. Now, drink!'

'I can't!' Sophie buried her face into her hands and began sobbing loudly. It was over. First Danny, now her. But it couldn't be. It couldn't end like his.

'You can and you will.' Zauberer jerked her head upwards and forced the glass to her mouth. Before Sophie could think, her mouth was filled with a swirling bitterness, thick and sweet at the same time. Zauberer pushed her backwards, and she fell to the floor heavily.

Zauberer looked up to the ceiling as a gentle tapping sound played on the floorboards upstairs. It was over almost as quickly as it had started, but the noise was welcomed by Sophie, who lay almost lifeless, like a fallen statue. Muttering under his breath, he seemed distracted and looked up once more. A gentle 'tap tap' came again from the room upstairs followed by a soft, almost glittering sound that Sophie couldn't place. After glancing once more at Sophie, he swiftly climbed the staircase.

# CHAPTER 21

Sophie waited until he had gone and clambered to her feet. Looking around, she grabbed a coat made of thick dark velvets and scooped the glue-like liquid from her mouth, until she was sure the taste and texture had gone. The coat now resembled a dead animal covered in sticky blood after being flattened by a car. Sophie used the soft white hankerchief to rub the inside of her mouth more fully, behind each tooth, her cheeks, her tongue, her gums, until the inside of her mouth was dry and sore and the white cotton had taken on a grubby amber hue.

A wild scream flooded down the stairs. Zauberer could be heard, hurling around what seemed like verses, poetry, in a language she didn't recognise. Sophie listened, silently creeping to the bottom of the stairs. She heard another calm voice, that of Lawrence's, speaking in hushed tones through Zauberer's hysterical ranting. The shrieking verses continued, and Mrs Dawson's voice floated above this, a light whisper over Lawrence's continued words. She spoke of children and magic, wizardry and evil, over and over until all that could be heard were her whispers and Lawrence's soothing tones. Sophie waited a moment longer, then climbed the stairs, not daring to make a sound. Sure that Zauberer must still be up there, she curled in the stone archway at the top of the stairs, stretching forward to see what was happening.

Lawrence sat in a far corner of the shop, surrounded by the puppets that had earlier hung around the walls. They were propped up against each other, as if listening to Lawrence's every word. He addressed them as he talked of the end of their suffering. Mrs Dawson was carefully placing strange objects on shelves and on the floor as she continued to utter the phrases Sophie had heard before. Snakeskin, coloured stones, bright feathers, and yellow petals decorated much of the room now, some loose, some stacked inside glass containers of many shapes and sizes, and Sophie remembered the collection of items she had been given earlier that day. She heard her name being whispered.

'The potion, Sophie. We need the potion.' Lawrence smiled, before looking back to the puppets and continuing his speech.

Cautiously searching the room for Zauberer, Sophie made sense of the earlier chaos she had heard from the cellar by observing the upturned furniture, the smashed pottery and coloured glass fragments until she finally glimpsed the old wizard lying in a crumpled heap by his table, his eyes open and moving, his body as still as stone. He now laid victim to Holly's spell, similar, no doubt, to one he'd used on those poor children stolen through the years. Sophie no longer feared him. She ran down to the wooden case and pulled out two full bottles of the potion before running back to Lawrence, placing them by him, and hiding back safely at the top of the stairs.

Lawrence stood slowly, repeating each line of his spell. One by one, he placed the puppets, until a ring of wooden children surrounded the frozen frame of Zauberer. Mrs Dawson joined in with Lawrence chanting a rhythm of sounds, not words Sophie had heard before, as they dragged the wizard into a sitting position. Sophie saw Zauberer's eyes dart frantically, as his body remained paralysed. Terrified, Sophie retreated back down two steps, feeling somehow protected by the space she allowed herself, yet compelled to watch, to see what would become of this evil creature.

Lawrence took the potion and twisted free the crystal stopper. The two whispered so quietly that Sophie couldn't hear what was being said. Watching, transfixed, she saw Mrs Dawson pull Zauberer's head back and force open his mouth, her face grim and determined.

The amber flowed freely, an endless stream of silent, sparkling fluid which disappeared down Zauberer's throat until the crystal vessel was empty.

What happened next was more than Sophie had ever imagined she'd see with her own eyes. Zauberer fell into the depths of the circle and lay motionless, his eyes now closed. The room seemed very still, echoing its emptiness, its silence, as if time itself had stopped.

Then, in an instant, turquoise, silver, and pearl sparks of light floated upward from the bodies of the child puppets, until a shimmering sheet of tiny stars hung poised over the lifeless wizard. His body glowed in the reflected light and in that glow, Zauberer's body turned slowly from leathery skin to tight carved wood, his cheekbones became hollow, his fingers jointed and twisted. The light danced around him, swirling round and round, and as a whirlpool spins down, down, down, the lights pulled Zauberer into them, making him smaller and smaller, until all that remained of him was a puppet, identical in every way to the original Zauberer, yet now the size of the empty crystal bottle.

Sophie stared, transfixed, as she saw silver cords twisting their way from upturned jars across the room to secure themselves painfully through Zauberer's wrists and ankles. Hazel driftwood scratched over the floorboards towards the centre, allowing themselves to be gently harnessed by the silver cord. The sparkling light rested above its creation. The puppet was complete.

Mrs Dawson moved over to Lawrence whose frame sat hunched by the circle of child puppets.

'Goodbye, Brother,' she whispered, her cheeks stained with tears. 'It is over.'

With that, she stood and motioned to the door, which opened effortlessly. 'Farewell, restless spirits,' she called to the sparkling light above the child puppets. 'Be at peace, my angels.'

The lights glittered, separating and filling the room with their glow. All at once, they moved through the door and drifted upwards until the dawn sky was filled with a shimmer of coloured silvers before becoming part of the fading moonshine.

Sophie stared out until the sky had returned to its purple candyfloss dawn. She touched her face and found it wet with tears. Mrs Dawson sat down by her and held her until she stopped sobbing.

As she looked round, she saw a figure curled in the far corner of the room.

'Lawrence?' Sophie spoke gently. She crawled over to where the sleeping figure lay and tapped him. The boy turned painfully and sat up.

'Danny!' Sophie put her arms gently around him and held him tightly.

'Sophie?' He looked up to Mrs Dawson and rubbed his face, sleepily.

Mrs Dawson walked over. 'We had better get home before morning.'

'I thought you were gone, Danny,' Sophie whispered, realising she had begun to cry again.

'I don't know what happened. Why are you here?'

Mrs Dawson helped Sophie and Danny to their feet. 'You were very lucky, my dear. Zauberer imprisoned you, as he had so many others. You entered his shop of your own free will and accepted his invitation to drink,' she continued, pointing to the crystal bottle on the floor.

'I did? Danny frowned, shaking his head. 'I don't remember.'

Sophie put her arms around her friend and squeezed him tightly. 'Zauberer hypnotised the children, Danny, he hypnotised you. I tried to help you, but I was too late.'

'On the contrary, my dear.' Mrs Dawson smiled, 'you saved Danny. Without your help, we would have seen Zauberer increase his collection with Danny, and perhaps move on to some other unsuspecting place.'

Sophie shuddered as she recalled being alone in the shop with him, of how afraid she was, of how terrified she became.

Mrs Dawson turned to Danny. 'This is quite remarkable, Danny. You have returned to your former self. How many glasses of the potion did you drink?'

Danny frowned, his face flickering with unsettled memories. 'I remember drinking from one glass. It was thick, like treacle. I don't know what happened after that . . .'

'You cannot have taken a full glass, Danny. Your fate would have been that of Lawrence's if you had drained one glass. He was trapped at that time, and so today, his spirit is free, and he, at last, is at rest.'

'Will Danny be all right, Mrs Dawson?' Sophie whispered. 'Will he go through what Lawrence . . . ?'

'You are a lucky young man,' she said, gently, rubbing her fingers through Danny's tousled hair. 'Zauberer's powers are gone, and you were not fully bewitched by him. The children stolen away drank two goblets of the potion. They are gone, but their spirits are free now, that at least is a blessing. The memories of this day will be with you always, but his evil spell will not.'

Dusting her clothes free of the sawdust and wood shavings, Sophie smiled and looked round. She walked to the door. 'Where is Lawrence?'

Mrs Dawson's shoulders slumped quietly. 'With the angels, Sophie. With the angels.'

Sophie gazed round at the empty shelves and floorboards. The silence that filled the empty spaces was calm and tranquil, so different from what she had come to expect from this strange place. Her heart felt heavy as she thought of Lawrence and the other children Zauberer had taken.

Mrs Dawson picked up the one remaining puppet and smiled sadly. 'We know just the place for you, Zauberer.'

After pulling the door securely closed behind them, the three trod silently back to the slowly stirring guest house.

# CHAPTER 22

The seagull's morning chorus woke Sophie from a deep, deep sleep. Opening her eyes, a bright daylight filled her room, and a salt breeze gently tickled her nostrils. Realising she was not alone, she focused on Danny and Nina sat at the end of her bed. For a moment, eyes tightly shut, she recalled the previous night's events and wondered for a moment if she had only dreamed the fantasy that had unfolded. Now, safely tucked up in her flowery quilt, it seemed so very far away, the smell of sawdust a fading memory.

The cries of seagulls outside her bedroom window pulled her back into the present. As her eyes opened again and caught Danny looking straight at her, his smile said it all.

'Good morning, sleepy.' Danny smiled.

Nina stood up, putting her arms affectionately around her brother's neck. 'Come on, we'll be late for breakfast. We all slept in this morning!'

Sophie smiled and got out of bed, amazed to see that she was dressed in her pyjamas.

They tumbled down to the dining room where Mum and Auntie Penny sat chattering with cups of tea.

'Well, look who it is,' Sophie's mum laughed. 'We thought we were having a child-free morning!'

Sophie sat down and looked around at her family. Mum. Auntie Penny. Nina. Danny. She smiled and reached for the teapot. Hearing everyone plan their final day on the beach, she wondered if she and Danny would ever be able to recover from events of the last few days.

'This will be our last 'Good morning, my dears!' from old Mrs Dawson,' Auntie Penny whispered.

Sophie snapped away from her thoughts and looked over to the doorway. Mrs Dawson stood in her usual black, silver hair arranged in the familiar knotted bun.

'Good morning, my dears,' she smiled as she walked towards them. Putting her hand on Sophie's shoulder, she spoke again. 'And how are you today?'

'Fine thank you, Mrs Dawson',' Sophie smiled. 'Everything's fine.'

'I've got something to show Danny and Sophie. Would you mind if I borrowed them for just a moment?'

Following Mrs Dawson through the hallway and into her own room, the two walked behind in silence. 'Now then, my dears,' she smiled, pointing to a distant corner of her room. 'I thought you would like to see this before you leave.'

In the corner stood Mrs Dawson's old wooden dresser with clear glass doors; an arrangement of ornaments of every shape and size adorning the shelves. Placed in the centre, sat a new addition. The puppet of Zauberer, his eyes staring out sadly from behind the glass.

'Safe,' she said, placing her hand for a moment on Danny's shoulder, 'where I will always be able to keep my eye on him.' Mr Zauberer's defeated gaze stared out at them, his eyes still as hollow as ever, although now without power or danger.

'Thank you for everything, Mrs Dawson,' Sophie whispered, staring into the cabinet, not knowing if she dare mention the events of the previous night.

'We worked together, Sophie. You were as much a part of it as dear Lawrence and me.'

'What about Lawrence?' Sophie asked.

Mrs Dawson put her arm around Sophie and hugged her gently. 'We will be reunited some day, Sophie. We are all reunited in the end. And while we are apart, I'm sure he will take care of us wherever he may be.' Mrs Dawson seemed sad and quiet for a moment.

Danny broke the silence. 'Thank you, Mrs Dawson. I still don't know what went on there, but I know you both probably saved my bacon!'

The three laughed together, and Sophie felt relief that the whole affair was now over.

Danny tugged playfully at Sophie's arm, pulling her away. 'Come on, Sophie. We'd better get back.'

Sophie looked back at Mrs Dawson, aware that Danny would never know the true depths of her friendship with this amazing old woman.

She walked quickly back to her dear, dear friend and they hugged tightly.

'Can I write to you?' Sophie asked.

'I would love that, Sophie. You take care now.' She pulled the amethyst and silver ring from her finger and held it out. 'Wear this, Sophie. You will always be in my thoughts.'

Sophie placed it on the first finger of her left hand and admired it closely. 'Mrs Dawson, it's beautiful. I will never forget you, you know.'

'I know, Sophie. Now, you both take care of yourselves,' she started, laying a hand on each child's shoulder. 'Danny, you have a good friend in Sophie. She has helped you in ways you will never know.'

The two children smiled at each other, and Danny gave Sophie an affectionate nudge. They all laughed, and the world somehow seemed brighter again.

'Now you had better run along,' she smiled, hurrying them out of her hallway in that brisk manner they remembered from their early meetings. 'Goodbye, my dears. Your world awaits!'

As Sophie left the guest house that afternoon, her amethyst ring glinting in the sunlight, she felt life would never be quite the same again. But she knew in her heart that whatever happened, Mrs Dawson and Lawrence would be there, protecting and guiding her for always.

# Author Notes

Driftwood & Amethyst is a fantasy story, infused with elements of magic realism and is Kate's first published novel. Kate found her inspiration from bygone family holidays in North Yorkshire and Northumberland, and more recently visiting seaside towns in North Yorkshire and on the Norfolk coastline with her new little family.

After writing in her spare time for as long as she can remember, Kate now writes full time producing educational and child development articles, primary teaching materials, short stories and poetry.

Now living in South Yorkshire, Kate is currently working on a whole array of stories and articles and is in the throes of her next children's novel.

Lightning Source UK Ltd.
Milton Keynes UK
UKOW02f0353111114

241425UK00002B/77/P